THE ROLES

We Play

JOANNA GRACE

A Division of Y&R Enterprises, LLC
PO Box 2283
Lindale, TX 75771

Cover Design by Once Upon A Time Covers
Book Design by Champagne Formats

Printed in the United States of America

Library of Congress Control Number Data
Grace, JoAnna.
   The roles we play / JoAnna Grace.
1.   Celebrity romance—Pregnancy—Fiction. 2. Romance—Contemporary—Fiction.
   Fiction. | BISAC: FICTION / Romance / Contemporary. | FICTION / Romance / General.
PCN # 2016911653 2014

ISBN 978-1-940460-07-9
ISBN 978-1-940460-08-6 (e-book)

www.authorjoannagrace.com
www.yandrpublishing.com

JoAnna Grace

BY JOANNA GRACE

Dedication & Acknowledgements

Thanks to the following:

A special thanks to Matt, whose "encounter" at the airport gave me the inspiration for this story. Love ya, oh great bald one. To my Mananda, a bestie who became family and we didn't even know it. Thanks for being my first writing partner and one of my first fans. Hugs and love to you and your family.

To my family, for allowing me to indulge in my writing passion. Thanks for letting me sleep in after working all night and forgiving me when I'm mentally on another planet. I love you!

To my Executive Council and friends: Mom, Cheryl, Anna, Jen, Connie C., and Chrissy, for your insight into this story. You guys are brilliant and wonderful.

To John, for your assistance along the way. You rock.

To my stupendous husband, who supports my wild ideas and goes with the flow. Have I told you lately?

Chapter One

KELLY ROLLED OVER in bed and picked up her cell phone. Mark's face smiled back at her as his Bon Jovi ringtone blared. What could he possibly want at three in the morning? Was he insane?

"You'd better be bleeding, jackass," she mumbled.

His deep chuckle filled the silence of her studio. "Damn, you're grumpy in the morning."

"It's not morning yet. It's that time of day even Jesus hates. What do you want? Where are you?"

"I had to work the late shift, remember?"

Kelly vaguely recalled that the night guy at the airport had quit and Mark had to fill in for him for a couple weeks. "I'm really sorry for your luck. Again, what do you want?"

"I need a favor."

Ah hell. The last time Mark needed a favor, Kelly ended up watching three little girls—scratch that, three little terrorists—all under the age of six so he could go bang their mom. "If this involves you getting laid, I'm not interested. Try that website for nanny services."

"Don't be bitter. It doesn't suit you."

"Point, Mark. Let's get to the *point*." She rubbed a hand over her messy hair and down her face. People should not be awake at three a.m., especially people like her.

"Remember that actor that had his plane serviced a couple months ago?"

Kelly answered with a grunt. She had to admit, it was pretty sweet that Mark had spent an entire afternoon chauffeuring around a big time celebrity while his plane was checked out. They went to lunch and spent the afternoon driving around and chatting like old friends. That was just Mark, though. He had the best luck of any person she'd ever met.

"We were having lunch and he starts telling me that he likes to hide out, right. No cameras, no interviews, just shootin' the shit. We got along, so I offered for him to stay around here when he needed to."

Kelly cursed. She knew exactly what Mark had offered. "What did you promise and how screwed am I?"

"Let me finish." Mark sighed, his nerves clearly shot. "So I *might* have led him to believe that I knew someone with a private bed and breakfast type place that is way off in the hills."

"Damn it, Mark. You know Pops doesn't like strangers."

"Well, here's the thing. He might have told his girlfriend about this little hidey-hole."

Kelly groaned. "Might have? God, you make me want to hold your head under water until the bubbles quit."

"Plane lands in an hour, private runway H."

Kelly was already pulling on her jeans because this was Mark. Even though Mark was a pain in the ass, he would give his left nut for her. "Do you mean to tell me that now I have to play hostess to some stuck up actress in hiding because she's in trouble and needs her publicist to smooth things over?"

"You know I love you, right?"

"Ha! This is why I don't do the whole *love* thing. Men

2

are pigs."

"All but me, babe. You're a freaking angel. Private run—"

"Runway H, got it, got it. Bye."

Kelly stood in the hangar at four in the morning. She was freezing. The November winds cut through her hoodie down to her bones. The private runways on this side of the small airport were lifeless. If this was another one of Mark's jokes, she would hang him and beat him like a dirty rug.

Mark enjoyed playing jokes, particularly on her.

As unfair as it was, he had to be the luckiest guy on the planet. God only knew how many pictures he had with famous people who flew into the airport and happened to land in the private hangar where he worked. The photos lined his wall. Movie stars, rock stars, even a porn star. Kelly didn't ask how he knew who she was. Some things needed to remain a mystery between friends.

The likelihood of this being real was high. As a small plane came in for a landing, Kelly took out her phone to see exactly who she was hosting.

"Mark?"

"That's his plane."

"*His* plane. It's a guy? You said your friend told his girlfriend."

Mark chuckled mischievously. "And she turned around and told her friend—an actor."

"Why won't you tell me who he is? Is this one of your pranks?" Kelly looked around, expecting to find Mark watching and laughing. "I will have your testicles."

"No pranks. This is honest to God the luckiest day of your life."

"Come on, Mark. Seriously, will I even recognize this guy? Have I seen any of his movies? What is he, extra number one hundred and fifty—" She stopped mid-sentence when her eyes locked on to the man stepping out of the private jet. "Holy. Shit. Please tell me that is not…"

"Your very own guilty pleasure, Trevor Jacobs. Happy Thanksgiving, Merry Christmas, and Happy Birthday for the next twenty years."

"If you ever need a kidney, I'm your girl. Gotta go." She hung up to Mark laughing and saying, "You're welcome."

Kelly watched her ultimate celebrity crush shoulder a duffle bag and head in her direction.

Damn, he was even hotter in person. From the first time she'd seen him on the big screen, Kelly had been a closet junkie. He was the definition of gorgeous. Tall, lean but built, dark hair, brown eyes that made her libido stand up and salute. Those eyes were as famous as his name. Women had been arrested for trying to sneak in to his hotels, hack his social media accounts, and track his cell phone. Not that Kelly was that obsessed—well, she was, just not in a *get-out-the-straightjacket* way.

But she remembered from an interview that he preferred when women didn't act crazy. He'd insisted that he was just another guy who enjoyed hamburgers and lazy Sundays.

Yeah. Just another guy with the body of a god, the face of an angel, lips of sin, and a voice that made her knees weak.

Yep, he could enjoy a burger at her place on Sundays all he wanted…as long as he did it naked.

"You Kelly?" asked a baritone laced with honey and spice.

"Yep." Kelly stuck out her hand. "Nice to meet you." She tried not to even smile as he slid his warm hand into hers. Her heart fluttered fast as her brain stalled out.

"Trevor."

"Yep."

He stuck his hands in his pockets and rocked back on

his heels. "So." He smiled. "You're my ride?"

"Yep." Kelly nodded and Trevor chuckled.

He looked around at the dark and empty hangar. Clearly her lack of intellectual conversation made him uncomfortable. "Well this is the only bag I have. So…if you're ready?"

He was trying to set her at ease. All she did was nod and say, "Okay." Her sedan wasn't much, but it was clean and the interior was nice. It was nothing compared to the jet he had just flown in on. He couldn't really complain, right?

They rode in silence for a few minutes. Kelly had no idea what to say and the fragrance of him nearly made her drunk. It was sexy and sweet. If she licked his skin, would he taste the same?

"You in some kind of trouble?" The words spilled out of her mouth before she considered tact.

Trevor threw his head back and laughed. "Not exactly. But getting away for a while is a good idea. A friend told me about this place in the mountains that was nice and quiet."

"Okay."

"You don't believe me?" He looked over and smirked. Kelly shrugged. "Truth is I got caught selling drugs with a hooker in my hotel room. We tried to run from the cops, bad deal."

The inflection in his words made her turn to look at him. Never in a million years would she have agreed to this if—damn, he was pretty.

After a few seconds, a goofy grin spread across his face and he laughed. He was totally messing with her. "You should see your expression."

"You're one of the top paid actors in Hollywood. Naturally I should assume you're full of shit." Thank goodness it was dark and he couldn't see the bright red of her face.

TREVOR WAS ABSOLUTELY floored. Usually he didn't get this level of honesty, especially from women. This one didn't seem to care one bit about who he was.

"You don't believe I simply needed a break?"

After a deep exhale she tiled her head. "Nope. Not if you're flying in at four in the morning before the first commercial flights start. This wasn't a planned vacation. You're running."

Trevor nodded, seeing the logic in her words. "I'll admit, I did want to leave at night and it was last minute. I recently finished shooting one movie and the director was going to throw me right into another. I told them I needed time to look at the script before I agreed."

"You getting burned out, Hollywood?"

Trevor looked out the window at the forest as it passed by. "Yeah, I guess you could say that." He didn't want to think about it. It was easier to focus on his cute hostess. "Tell me about your place."

"Um, about that. Mark lied his ass off. I don't have a B and B."

That's kind of important since he was traveling to God only knew where. He cleared his throat. "Care to elaborate?"

"My grandfather owns a historical plantation house. It's been kept up quite well, and in our neck of the woods I guess you could call it a famous mansion. We usually don't keep guests."

"Mark said—"

"Yeah, I can imagine what Mark said and what it became by the time it hit your ears. It's fantastic; you won't be disappointed. There's not exactly a wait staff, so don't try to call in room service. Catch my drift?" Kelly yawned with a sigh. "Sorry, I'm not a morning person."

"Me either. And four thirty isn't morning. It's evil."

She laughed, actually laughed. It was a beautiful sound, slightly husky.

"I agree. I'll get you set up in a room and if you'll let me catch a couple hours of shut eye, I'll take you out for breakfast."

Trevor smiled. There was something refreshing about her honesty and outspokenness. She was *real*. It'd been a while since he'd been with a woman who was comfortable enough to call him out. Was there more to this woman? What made her act differently towards him?

Funny, he was rather excited to find out.

Kelly was right. The mansion was fantastic. Three stories of plantation perfection complete with white columns holding up the wrap-around balcony.

"Wow." He stepped out of the car and walked up the lit path. "You don't have weddings here?" He couldn't believe that a house so grand didn't get a lot of traffic. A place this majestic could be a gold mine.

"When my grandfather was a child, his parents threw parties. The place was crawling with people every night of the week." She didn't walk to the front door, but around to the side entrance of the mansion. "Turns out, his parents were both cheating and used the parties as cover for their affairs. When they found out, it tore their family apart. He was an only child so they lived together for his sake, but it was rough to say the least."

"That could screw with a kid. No need to carry on that tradition." Trevor nodded.

"Occasionally I do photo shoots. We have friends and certain family members that come and visit, but since it's just Pops and me left, we don't draw a big crowd."

Trevor followed closely as Kelly led him through the house, her voice lowering to a whisper. "We have one lady that keeps up the house as well as a gardener."

"Why don't you try to bring in more traffic? You could make a killing off this place," he whispered as they went up a set of old stairs that must have served as a staff entrance decades ago.

Kelly never stopped climbing the stairs. "People cause problems."

He couldn't argue about that. That's why he was here to begin with.

Chapter Two

KELLY SHOWED TREVOR to one of the larger guest rooms she knew had been tidied up within the last couple days. The antiques and plush bedding would suit him fine. This room also had one of the many hidden passageways around the house. It led to the ballroom that had been converted into her studio.

"I'll be back in a few hours and we can eat, okay?" She flipped on the light and let him in.

"Sure, okay." Trevor scanned the room, his mouth hanging slack. The way he slowly turned and examined the room allowed her time to get a good view of his muscular body.

Lord have mercy, she needed to get the heck out of this room.

"Well, goodnight then." She walked over to one of the wall panels by the fireplace and pulled down on the sconce. With a click, the panel snapped open.

"No *way*." Trevor opened the panel and stuck his head in the dark hall. When he looked back at Kelly, she nearly forgot to breathe. Heat from his body invaded her personal space. His eyes were childlike and his face was openly fascinated. "That's freaking awesome. Where does it go? Show me."

Damn it! How could she possibly say no to that face, those bedroom eyes, those lips?

"Okay, but after that I'm going to bed and you can find your own damn way back up here." She slipped into the thin passage and pulled the string that lit a single bulb. It was musky and dark despite the light. They went down a staircase and took a right where the passage branched off.

"This is so damn cool. You could give tours."

"Easy there, big guy." Kelly laughed. "We like our privacy."

"It's a shame you don't share this with people. I get the need for privacy, probably more than most, but this is a historic building."

"Exactly. It's being preserved by the people who love it most. No one else would care the way we do. Having people in and out would add to the needed maintenance. Besides, I do photo shoots in the gardens all the time. That's enough." Kelly reached her studio and turned to dismiss Trevor. For reasons she didn't dare think about, she wanted him to see more of her home. "This used to be the ballroom. It's my studio now."

With the turn of a knob, she and Trevor walked into her gargantuan bedroom. She flipped on the lights and was grateful that she was a neat freak. Only her pajamas were out of place, and that was because she'd changed in a hurry. They were thrown across her bed.

Trevor let out a whistle. "Now this is a bedroom." Hands in his pockets, he spun around in the middle of the room and checked it out. "My entire apartment could fit in here."

"No mansions, Hollywood?"

He shook his head. "Nope. I have a couple places though. One in New York, one in Cali."

Figures.

This room was her sanctuary. It was the one place in the house her grandfather had agreed to give her full control of decorating and keeping up. Kelly had kept it in pristine condition. When her time here was up, the next owners wouldn't appreciate it if she destroyed the historic quality of the room. The walls remained white with intricate gold leaf patterns around the trim. The elegant chandelier had been fixed multiple times, but still hung in the center of the rectangle-shaped room. At the south end was her photography studio and work place. The antique desk had been moved from another room of the house along with the winged back chairs and coffee table that made up a small sitting area.

The north end of the room was sectioned off by heavy white drapes. Pops had allowed her to rig the curtain to substitute building a wall. Naturally, because that was the one place she didn't allow visitors, it was right where Trevor wanted to snoop.

He cleared his throat. "Wow."

Kelly's face grew warm. "I know. I have girly tastes."

The tall canopy bed was draped in more white, a stark contrast to the black bed frame and headboard. Kelly had splurged on Egyptian cotton sheets and the finest quality down blankets. Luxurious pillows were piled high. While the rest of the studio had the original hardwood floors, various rugs were layered on one another to create a cushion of white, gold, and black designs around her bed.

"No, it's, it's—" He walked slowly to the bed, touched the black metal frame and glanced over at her. "It's a very sexy bed."

Kelly swallowed. The way he drew out those words flooded her mind with erotic images of tangled sheets and sweaty bodies. How was she supposed to respond? Here was her favorite celebrity crush, in her bedroom, touching her sheets and telling her how *sexy* her bed was.

She had to be dreaming.

A painful bite of her tongue didn't cause her to wake up.

Nope, this was really happening. And it needed to stop.

"It's also very comfortable, which is why I'd like to get back to it. Please," she added for politeness.

Trevor smirked. He knew what he was doing to her and that only sparked her defiant side.

"Good night then." Trevor nodded and went back to the hidden door. Just before he closed the panel on the wall he took one last sweep of the space until his eyes landed on her. "Sweet dreams."

"They can't be any sweeter than this reality," she whispered to the empty room. "Mark's going to be hell to live with now."

A COUPLE OF hours later and Trevor was still unable to sleep. What was he doing here? Why the hell did he run out on everyone? More importantly, why did he have Kelly's brown eyes stuck in his mind?

The things he'd yelled at his publicist and agent were going to require apologies when he got home. He made a note on his phone to buy them gifts. They never stayed mad when he bought them things and he kind of resented them for that.

It got old being around people he could simply buy off. They weren't his real friends. They said things like, "We only want what's best for you," and "We care about your happiness." He didn't doubt that. The things that made him happy made his entourage rich. The things that were *best* for him in their eyes were the jobs that lined their pockets.

His old acting coach had called it a necessary evil. Boy, had he been right. Even as Trevor lay there despising them, the notifications on his phone kept popping up. Texts, emails, tweets, messages on Facebook. Where did he go? What was wrong? Was he on drugs? Did he need the name of a rehab facility? Was he coming back for some party next week? Did he have a secret lover they needed to pay off?

He finally turned the damn thing off. The script he was supposed to review was in his duffle, and it was going to stay there. When his agent had first proposed it, she'd promised it would benefit his career to take on an "edgier, sexier role." Like he needed a boost. His net worth was skyrocketing with bigger and better offers that came in daily; every brand of high dollar merchandise from socks to cologne to food wanted him as their spokesperson.

It was impossible to do something as simple as buy groceries. Standing in line for milk was becoming a test of local law enforcement. How fast could they pull a crazy woman off him?

He rolled to his side and sighed. Was this it? Was this really what he wanted out of his acting career? Out of his *life*? Things hadn't started out down this path and now he was losing control all together. Wasn't he?

What about Kelly and her grandfather? If he had a heart at all, he would leave them in peace. Once word got out that he was here, their private lives were gone too. The idea of somehow bringing discomfort to his hostess triggered a pain in his chest.

It said something that Kelly had jumped out of bed in the early morning hours, waited in the cold for a complete stranger, and given him such sweet digs to stay in. Sure, she'd done it for this Mark fellow. It still showed her loyalty. What did a man have to do to find loyalty so deep? Were Kelly and Mark lovers? Family?

He smiled thinking about how her eyes had been wide as dinner plates when she recognized him at the airport, and again when he called her bed sexy. It *was* sexy. The mental image of her in it was sexy, too.

That was something he'd pay to see. Kelly's naked body reclined on the bed, her golden hair spread over those white pillows, her back arching upwards while her legs wrapped around his waist.

Jeez, now he was hard. He forced himself to calm down. The sun was almost up and he couldn't have Kelly see him like this. Forget sleep. Instead of staring at the ceiling, he rolled out of bed and went into his kickboxing warm ups. He tried not to think about feminine brown eyes and her husky voice.

It didn't work.

Chapter Three

KELLY WOKE JUST before nine. It took her a moment to remember what she'd done last night and who was upstairs.

"Oh my God." She kicked off her covers and went to shower faster than a late bride. Her hair went into a haphazard bun with tendrils falling out everywhere but she didn't care.

Trevor Jacobs would be expecting breakfast and—wait. There was something else she had to do today. What was it?

Laughter down the hall snapped her back to attention. In her dining room, happily having breakfast, she found Mark, Trevor, and Pops.

"Morning, babe." Mark grinned. He stood to press a kiss to her cheek, something he usually did when she'd saved his ass.

"Hey." Kelly gave him a glare that no one else seemed to catch.

"Kelly, dear, you sure did sleep late."

"Sorry, Pops." She bent to kiss his bald head. "Guess I didn't sleep well."

"Mark brought breakfast. I was going to wake you, but he suggested letting you sleep. Come sit and eat." Pops stood to pull out a chair for her. His movements betrayed his usual morning stiffness. Each day she noticed it more. Each day she wished he would go see a specialist. Arthritis was his cover for something bigger. Stubbornness was a family trait.

Kelly felt Trevor's eyes on her, studying the family dynamic. Their eyes met and he returned her quick smile. "Good morning, Kelly."

"Sleep well?"

Politeness usually required coffee, but she forced the words. Mark handed her a huge cup with a Starbucks logo as if he'd read her mind. Kelly tasted the chocolate flavored delight and moaned in appreciation. "Oh, thank you, God."

"You can just call me Mark." He grinned and Trevor chuckled.

"Mark was telling me you're in films, Trevor," Pops said. "Any I might have seen?"

Mark leaned over and spoke loudly, "He's in moving pictures, Pops. Talkies."

"Shut your flapper, punk. I'm not deaf or dumb." Pops sneered. The banter between the two most important men in her life was comforting. If Trevor didn't catch the playful grins, he might have thought they hated each other.

"What movies?" her grandfather asked.

Trevor listed off three of his titles and Pop's white eyebrows rose high on his head. "My goodness, son. I know who you are." He extended his hand. "It's a pleasure to have you in our home. How did you end up meeting the bonehead over there?" He gestured to Mark.

Trevor smiled at Kelly when she rolled her eyes. "We have a mutual friend and she suggested this would be a good place for me to…rest a while."

"Good, good. Well, Kelly is a huge fan, did she tell you? She dragged me to that last movie of yours at least twice, saw it once with Mark, once with her girlfriends, again by her—"

"Pops," Kelly gasped. "He gets it." A fiery blush rushed up her neck, scorching her cheeks. She sipped her coffee and avoided Trevor's eyes.

"She didn't mention that, Pops. Thanks for filling me in." Trevor tilted his head at her. The smug bastard had the nerve to wiggle his brows suggestively.

"Oh yeah, she's even got a poster."

"Wow. It is time for a change of topic." Kelly rose to grab a croissant. "So, Mark, how's life at the airport?"

He laughed and talked around his food. "Not nearly as interesting as this conversation. Keep going, Pops."

As Pops launched into a story about the poster, Kelly heard the doorbell. "Thank you, Jesus. I'll get it." She all but ran from the room.

The couple standing at the door both wore stern expressions. *Shit!* That's what she was supposed to do today. Between Trevor Jacobs and a lack of sleep, her brain was fried.

"Ann. Gabe. Good morning." She was supposed to be doing their engagement photos at nine. It was nine-thirty. *Damn it.* Thank goodness she kept her equipment ready.

"Sorry we're late. But *someone* had to change clothes fifty times." Gabe extended a hand.

"These are our engagement pictures, *Gabriel.* Did you *want* to send three hundred of our not-so-closest friends pictures of us in our pajamas?" Ann stepped around him and into the foyer.

Kelly wished for a noose and a tall tree. *It's going to be one of those days.*

"What's *that* supposed to mean? Those people are business associates and friends." Gabe followed her in. "You're the one who wanted a big wedding."

As they grumbled about the guest list, Kelly asked them to take a seat in the parlor while she gathered her things—and dealt with the A-list celebrity who did not need to be seen by the town's two biggest gossips.

The three men hadn't left the dining room and were laughing, probably at her expense. But Trevor was telling a story.

"Then I went to stand up after falling on my ass and the towel got caught in the car door."

Trevor's captive audience of two roared. Mark threw back his head and Pop's bent over until she feared his dentures would fall out.

"So there I am in the middle of Manhattan, in nothing but a Speedo. Needless to say, my pictures were on every stalker website from here to Hong Kong in about three minutes. It was so damn cold I thought my balls were going to freeze off."

For a moment, she stood there and dissected the scene in front of her. It was nice to see Pops laughing and Mark wiping tears from his eyes. Trevor was grinning from ear to ear and her heart sputtered when he looked up at her and winked.

"Who was at the door, dear?" Pops asked in between deep breaths.

"My nine o'clock photo shoot. I completely forgot. I'm taking them to the water garden, so I'll be working for about an hour. Maybe longer cause they're bitching at each other. Not too conducive for engagement photos."

"No worries. I can keep the boy busy and out of sight." Pops waved her off.

Mark stood up and cleaned the dishes off the table. "I have to get some sleep. Mind if I grab a room upstairs?"

The men began to talk as if they forgot she was even there. "Okay then." She dashed back to her studio and grabbed her camera, laptop, and a light jacket.

Ann and Gabe sat on opposite sides of the room, her typing on the cell phone, him looking at a magazine. Kelly nearly laughed when she saw Trevor's picture on the front with the headline "Heartbroken or heartbreaker?"

"Why don't we head outside now?" She guided them through the back of the house and out into the gardens.

"It's so cold," Ann whined.

"If you had on warm clothes, you wouldn't be cold," Gabe snipped.

Kelly sighed. *Screw me sideways, I don't want to do this today.*

Ann narrowed her eyes at him. "We are having a spring wedding. We should be dressed appropriately."

"It's November, and there's snow on the ground. You think people won't notice that in the pictures?" Gabe pointed to all the white spots.

Before Ann could snap her retort, Kelly tried to defuse the situation. "Actually, the water gardens are a great place because we keep it cleared off and it's partially covered."

"*See,* Gabriel. I know what I'm doing. Megan and Richard had their pictures taken here and they were perfect."

"Well God knows we have to be as perfect as Megan and Richard." He rolled his eyes and crossed his arms over his chest.

Kelly took a deep breath as they bickered about keeping up with their socialite friends. She hadn't had near enough sleep or coffee to put up with this crap.

Twenty minutes into the shoot, they had a problem. Ann's smiles were fake and Gabe's eyes looked like he was half asleep. It didn't help that they didn't want to stand too close or hug or connect as couples in love should.

Under the guise of changing lenses, Kelly had everyone sit down under the pergola and take a break. "Gabe, tell me about the first time you met."

"Oh my God, please don't." Ann put a hand on her face.

For the first time since their arrival, a sincere smile creased Gabe's face. "We were at a club. Ann was drunk—"

"Tipsy."

"Drunk off her ass. She stepped out onto the dance

floor during a slow song and danced all alone."

Ann blushed and hid a grin.

"She swayed and was running her hands down her body." Gabe demonstrated and Kelly hid a smirk when Ann once again slapped a hand over her face.

"Okay, I might have been under the influence," Ann admitted, face the color of beets.

"Plastered," Gabe said and laughed. Ann batted at his arm affectionately, giggling along with him.

There. Now they were getting somewhere.

"How was she dancing, Gabe?" Kelly asked.

He stood and imitated his fiancée.

Ann laughed and swatted at him to sit down. It was rather comical. "It wasn't like that."

"It was close." Gabe sat back down and put his hand on her back. "Anyway, she's dancing all alone like a lunatic, and my friend dared me to go dance with her. I did, because she's totally hot." He gave a wistful sigh and looked into Ann's eyes. "I've been attached ever since. Given that she hurled on me, that's saying something."

"Back up, what?" Kelly kept them so engrossed in the story they didn't realize that she'd stood and led them back to the water gardens.

"I said I was sorry. I even sent him a fruit basket." Ann smiled genuinely for the first time.

"Chocolate covered fruit." Gabe rolled his eyes. "Perfect for the guy allergic to chocolate. Naturally I had to call and give her hell."

"He invited me to dinner and that was our first date."

Kelly snapped a picture of them smiling at one another and again when Gabe reached up and touched her cheek.

"You were the prettiest girl I'd ever seen. Even drunk, you took my breath away."

"Aw, Gabe." Ann pressed a kiss to his lips. Kelly snapped away until Ann realized she was taking pictures.

"Sorry, Kelly. Should we be posing?"

"Nope, keep talking. This is great stuff. What was the first thing that attracted you to Gabe?"

Ann tilted her head and the sun hit her curls just right. *Click.*

"I loved his shoulders. He pulled me against him while we danced and I remember thinking how strong and solid he felt."

"Show me," Kelly murmured, not wanting to break up the moment.

Ann stepped in to Gabe, and he held her close as she put her head against his shoulder.

Click.

They swayed and Kelly moved to get a shot from a higher position. Gabe's eyes were closed, lips pulled back, lost in the sweet memory.

Click.

Over the next half hour Kelly kept asking questions about what they loved about each other and snapping photos. She moved them about the fountains and flowing creek that wove around the estate.

The shots were great; Ann and Gabe were finally connecting.

By the end of the session, Kelly was confident she had good material to work with. She told them she'd take about a week to edit and put together a portfolio so they could choose their prints.

Before they left, she went to her studio and printed off one picture she thought was the best. The couple held each other, kissing. Ann clung to Gabe's shirt and his hands were crushed in her hair. The shot conveyed the passion and the desire that led them to get married.

"Here. I want you to have this."

Ann and Gabe both gasped at the shot.

"The next time you get caught up on who took longer to dress or who fills the seats at the wedding, remember this moment. Remember the love that brought you together. That's what's important."

The couple kissed before Gabe hugged Ann close.

"Thanks, Kelly. This has been a lot more fun than I expected."

Ann confirmed she would be the photographer at the wedding next spring, and Kelly showed them out.

Chapter Four

TREVOR HAD LAUGHED until his sides hurt. Pops was a nonstop comedy routine. No wonder Kelly was so protective of him. The old man was a riot. The ribbing between him and Mark, well, it couldn't be scripted. It would never be as funny on paper as it was watching the two go back and forth live.

The old man was inquisitive as hell. He wanted to know everything about Trevor, his family, his upbringing, what got him into "pictures." Trevor asked him a question that turned the tables.

"Pops, is, uh, is Kelly seeing anyone? I mean, she and Mark seem really close. Are they just friends?"

The question elicited an immediate change in the old man's face. He leaned back in his chair and his eyes were more alert. "Why do you ask?"

"Curiosity."

It took Pops a long time to answer, and Trevor knew he'd made a mistake.

"Listen closely, son. My granddaughter has a barrier that could rival the Great Wall of China around her. The only person she lets in is Mark. Even I'm standing on the outside. If you have plans of a conquest during this sabbatical of yours, find someone else. You're a nice fellow, but that battle will get bloody."

Pops patted Trevor's knee and stood up, grumbling about not being a young gun anymore. He left Trevor with directions to the solarium where he could watch the photo shoot.

That's where he ended up spying as Kelly worked with the arguing couple. As the shoot went on, he saw the transformation from anger to affection.

When she came back from showing them out, Kelly took a seat on a bench and watched the water. The look on her face reminded him of what Pops had said. He wanted to know how to breech that wall. Maybe it was the conquest. He always enjoyed a new challenge.

He opened the back door and stuck his head out. "*Pssst.*"

Kelly turned.

"Is it safe?"

She gave a one-shouldered shrug. "There're no dead bodies, so I guess."

Trevor joined her on the bench and admired the man-made water features. A creek started at a small waterfall about thirty yards away. The water wound around and ended up in a pond full of hand-crafted, blown glass fish. Each sliver of glass had colors melted into it making the school vibrant and beautiful.

"Those are interesting," he said.

"Thanks. I made them."

He caught her eye. "You work with glass too?"

"It's a hobby. Those are from stained glass windows I salvaged from an old church. This bench is made from the wood of their choir loft."

"Okay, I'm impressed. Carpenter, glass blower, photographer, marriage counselor, and you run a spectacular B and B." His heart softened when she blushed, her laughter laced with nervousness. "Anything else you're amazingly talented at?"

"Flattery will get you nowhere, Hollywood."

They shared a chuckle before she stood and grabbed her camera. "Would you like the grand tour?"

"If you leave the camera here." He'd developed a serious aversion to the damn things.

"Don't worry. Neither one of us wants people to know you were ever here. I like taking morning shots of the gardens. Around the east side of the house is a marvelous view of the valley."

They meandered in comfortable silence. He appreciated that about Kelly. She didn't fill the blank spaces with needless words. She was right; the east side of the property had a jaw-dropping view. Trevor walked over to a half-buried rock wall that had to be as old as the house. He propped up one leg and bent over with his elbows on his knee. A chilled breeze of fresh mountain air blew into his face and he closed his eyes to take in the stillness of the world about him. He shut everything out and his soul was calm.

No filming deadlines, no directors, no scripts he had to review. No agents and publicists pushing him every which way. He could enjoy the serenity of this place.

Click.

He snapped his face to Kelly, who shyly lowered her camera. Her eyes darted around avoiding his. "I'm sorry. You looked amazing in that shot." She realized what came out of her mouth and began to stutter. "I mean, you didn't look amazing. It was the view and the pose and the sunlight on your hair. And I'm going to shut up now. Sorry. I can delete it." She pressed a couple buttons on the camera.

"No, let me see the shot." He peered at the small screen on her fancy camera.

He'd been shot with every high-powered, high-priced camera in the world. Yet when he saw the picture she'd taken, he'd learned it was all about the photographer's eye. The shot *was* fantastic.

The sunlight bathed the world beyond him and hit the layer of fog on the valley just right. His eyes were closed, his face serene. Trevor wanted to remember that moment forever. And now he could.

"You're right," he whispered next to her ear. He leaned in over her shoulder. "It's amazing. I want a copy of it."

Kelly turned her face until they were within inches of one another. "You're not mad?"

"No. I want to see it blown up."

The world stopped and his eyes flickered down to her plump lips. What would she taste like? Would she melt him with her lips the way she was with her eyes?

Kelly didn't give him the chance to find out. She stepped away and turned her back. "I need to go load the shots from this morning into my computer. Make yourself at home." She scurried back into the house and left him in the yard.

What they hell was he doing? If he had one rule in his life, it was to never get involved with a woman like Kelly. She was the kind that did damage, the kind you fell for and had to leave. He stuck to the Hollywood girls who didn't have a brain in their heads. They didn't ask questions, they didn't care about his inner values or think of the future. Too preoccupied with parties, spray tans, and hair appointments.

Kelly didn't fit that mold. She didn't even wear make-up. She was skilled at a myriad of things. She was the kind of beautiful that seeped from the inside out, walled heart or not.

KELLY LEANED OVER her computer and compared

the lighting in two photos. The canvas-covered patio had diffused some of the morning sun, but a couple rays made it into the shots. To anyone else the two shots would have been identical. She agonized over the details. It was what made her a good photographer. It was what kept her sane and grounded in every other aspect of her life.

As much as she tried to distract herself with the pictures, the momentum was lost when the final picture popped up on the screen.

Trevor.

"Damn it." She closed the laptop and put her hands over her eyes. Had she really nearly kissed him this morning? Was she absolutely off her rocker? Getting involved with a celebrity wasn't smart. *Not in any way, shape, or form.*

She had read the magazines, seen the interviews, and watched his career over the last couple years. Trevor was a ladies' man and the tabloids loved to track his flavor of the week.

Kelly could *not* let herself get swept away by a pretty face. *Been there, done that.*

"Hey babe." Mark came through the door of her room without knocking. He was donning his jacket and adjusting his collar. "How's it going?"

"Great," she lied.

"Cool. Well, I've got to go take care of things at home before work this evening. You good to go?"

"Yep."

Mark stopped in his tracks. "Uh-oh. You only say it like that when you're hiding something. Is it Trevor? Is he too much to handle?"

If he only knew. "No, he's been a perfect house guest. I'm still tired, I guess."

Mark nodded, pursing his lips. "You'd tell me if something was wrong, right?"

"Yep."

"Liar."

"Asshat."

Mark laughed and kissed her forehead. "I'll call you later. I have a short shift since I covered last night. You want to do movies and pizza later?"

"Sure, let's watch a Trevor Jacobs film and see if he squirms."

"I love that evil streak in you." Mark winked and bustled out the door.

Kelly hid in her room until lunchtime. She figured it would be rude not to check on her guest and feed him. She found Trevor sitting in the parlor looking over a thick pile of papers. Deep in her gut, butterflies flapped their wings, and she hated the thought of it.

"Hey," she said, coming up behind him.

"Hey." He popped to his feet. Papers fell from his hands and he scrambled to pick them up. "Sorry, I was engrossed and I didn't hear you."

"My fault. What do you have there?" She bent to help him clean up.

"The script for my next movie. I'm supposed to start shooting next month and I don't know if I—" He looked into her eyes. "Never mind. It's not important."

"Sure it is. How about I grab some lunch and you can tell me about it."

His brows dipped. "Really?"

No doubt, she was a glutton for punishment. "Yeah, I'd love to be a springboard if you need one."

What the hell was she saying? *Shut it, Kelly.*

"Great. I'd like a woman's opinion."

"Okay then." She retreated to the kitchen to make lunch. One day she might learn how to speak to him like she had an entire brain and knew how to form complete sentences.

Curiosity was a dangerous thing. But she wanted to

be the person he discussed this project with. When would she ever have this chance again? Who in their right mind wouldn't want to talk movies with their favorite movie star? It would be like sitting down with her favorite author and talking about books or sitting down with her favorite photographers and swapping tips.

She took the peanut butter from the cabinet and looked at the smiling figure on the front as he touched his top hat. "Yep, you and I are both nuts. Can you say, *hello justification*?"

Chapter Five

KELLY PRESENTED HIM with a wonderful, simple lunch. Sandwiches and fruit were about all his stomach could handle anyway. Sharing the script with her made Trevor's stomach roll over, which made no sense. He'd stood on stage at awards shows and felt calmer than he did when she brought out the tray of food.

She sat across the room and picked at her grapes while reading over the screenplay. This was the first time he'd reviewed it. He read a page and handed it to her. She was quicker than he was because he often looked up to see her hand waving on another page.

Impatient little thing, aren't you?

As with the last two movies he'd been in, the plot didn't thrill him. What would she think? They sat in silence for a long time while she read. The only sound was rustling pages. They rested against her knee, her leg curled up in the chair with her.

Trevor tried to pretend to read, but he couldn't stop watching her out of the corner of his eye. Her light-colored brows stayed dipped low as her brown eyes went from left to right, line by line. Take another page. Read more. Frown. Cringe. Get another page.

The hands on the grandfather clock circled around and around. They only spoke when he offered to refill her glass and switch on a couple of lamps.

Finally, as the sun set, she closed the pages and plopped it down on the table.

"Wow." She blew out a heavy breath and stood up to stretch her body. Her body curved in all the right places, a bit thicker around the thighs and chest. Raising her arms above her head, she stretched her back and gave him a fantastic view of her butt. Images of what he could do with those curves ran through his mind.

The lusty feeling didn't last long. When she turned around, she crossed her arms over her chest and stared down at him. "What did you think of it?"

"I think it will sell tickets. This type of thing seems to be popular right now."

"No, I mean what did you think about the characters, the plot, the overall message?"

She was fishing for something, but what? "I think the main character is a jerk. Women are somehow attracted to jerky types. The sexual stuff is appealing to women. It's going to stretch me to pull this off. I don't know much about dominants and their submissives, but—"

"This doesn't seem like something you would normally do. Is that why you're doing it? To stretch yourself?" Her voice was even, but her body shook.

"Not really. My agent thought I needed something different and this is very different. It happens to be a popular—"

"Popular subject, yeah. I know." She looked down at the floor.

The whole movie revolved around a couple that dives into the world of BDSM. As they get deeper, he becomes more and more aggressive. It turns out he likes to hurt women. The leading lady is cheated on, abused, and eventually leaves her husband of ten years.

"I've barely known you for a day, but I can already tell by your body language and your eye movements that you have something to say about this screenplay. Just say it."

"It's terrible." She threw her hands up in the air. "Are you seriously going to portray this asshole? As a fan, I want to beat you senseless for even considering it. It's vulgar and trashy and I can't imagine it's rated PG thirteen." Her voice grew louder as she griped at him.

"R."

"See. You have young fans too. You can't possibly think they won't sneak in to see this simply because their favorite badass movie star is in it. Would you want a teenager to watch what this script has you doing to this woman? And even worse, getting away with it? The lead character suffers no consequences for his actions. There's no responsibility or accountability for his behavior. His wife leaves, end of story. No big deal."

"Kelly, it's just a character, it's not really me." He rose to meet her face-to-face.

"You have to know that people will associate this character with you for the rest of your career. He's a controlling, manipulative monster that gets to continue on his merry way hurting women." She shook harder and her bottom lip trembled. "And the woman, come on." She picked up the script and turned to a page and began quoting the script. " '*He ties her wrist so tight her fingers go numb and he then whips her until she sobs.*'" She threw the papers down on the table. "That doesn't have the markers of a serial rapist *at all*." Sarcasm was alive and pulsating in her words. "I don't get it. You're always the good guy. You're the hero who beats the odds to save the girl, and save the world, and achieve the unachievable. Why would you lower your standards to portray this filthy vermin of a man? For more money? You said it yourself, this subject is really popular. You feel like you need to sell your soul?"

There was more at stake here than his reputation or his pocketbook. "Kelly." He reached for her hand, but she pulled away.

"You know what? Screw it. You do what you want."

Once again he was left in her wake. He flopped down in the chair and rubbed his forehead. Yeah, he agreed that this character was less than ideal. But there had been worse men on the big screen. This movie was going to be loaded with all the things that sold tickets: the romance of the couple, the kinky sex they explore, not to mention the guy's obsession with the woman. Chicks loved that crap. This movie was projected to be one of the best selling tickets of the year.

So why didn't he care more?

What he did care about was why Kelly had been so upset. *Overly upset.*

He went downstairs and to the other side of the house to her studio. He saw Pops coming out of her room and closing the door. The old man's sharp eyes pinned him.

"Can I help you, son?"

"I need to speak with Kelly. Excuse me."

He was surprised at Pops' grip as he caught his arm. "I don't think that's a good idea. There was still a bit of power left in the old man. Trevor had to respect that.

"She's really upset, isn't she?"

"Let's take a walk. She needs a moment." Pops gave a tight-lipped nod and Trevor followed him out to the solarium. They sat down and Pops sighed. "Why don't you tell me what happened? I couldn't get much from her."

Trevor gave him the rundown of the afternoon. He described the screenplay and her reaction to it. "I don't understand what I did wrong. She just doesn't get it. This film could do wonders for my career. Sure, it has some distasteful moments, but sex sells and this movie is all about it."

"Is that what matters to you, Trevor? How many tickets

a film sells?"

Trevor shrugged. "It pays the bills, you know."

"What I'm hearing is, all you care about is money. That's nice and shallow of you."

So much for not being defensive. "Hey, don't be so judgmental."

"Son, I've got underwear older than you. I've lived for over seventy years, fought in wars, buried a son, a daughter-in-law, and the only woman I ever loved and had relations with, raised an orphan grand daughter, and lived through my other son being a total waste of space. I've seen it all, done most of it, and walked away from more trouble than I care to count." He leaned over, his eyes narrowed. "I'll be as judgmental as I damned well please and you're not going to say nothing else about it. Punks like you are a dime a dozen. What makes you so special?"

Trevor could only stare. How do you argue with that? Compared to his man, he was, well, not all that impressive. He opened his mouth to speak twice and shut it. "It's not all about the money." It even sounded lame to him. "I care about my career, my image."

"And what about your integrity?" Pops questioned, the softness of his voice easing the sting of the words.

Trevor tried not to react defensively. "With all due respect, sir, I have a good reputation. I don't get into legal trouble or anything. I'm clean. Not many of my fellow actors can say that. Hell, some build an empire around their lack of integrity."

Pops nodded. "True, true. I'll admit I'm a bit behind on what's *hip* with the kids today. But there is one thing that I know stands the test of time. Perception."

"Sir?"

"How people perceive you. This movie sounds like the kind of thing that will surely make you more money. But it will also cause people's perception of you to change. Women will wonder if this is the lifestyle you are into. Men will think it's acceptable because you act it out. And then there are people like my Kelly." He took a deep breath and let it out with a sigh. "Who have lived a similar nightmare."

Trevor's throat closed up and he felt dizzy.

"Her perception of you will change. As will that of millions of other women who have been abused by manipulative men. You see, son, you were wrong about one thing. She does get it. She gets it all too well."

Trevor leaned over his knees and hung his head. One of the reasons he was okay with this film was because it was disconnected from his reality. He didn't know anyone who participated in the lifestyle, didn't know the real meaning of the traditions or rules. Sure, he would have done his research to accurately portray the part. Until that moment, when the concept was attached to an individual he had shared a meal with, it was foreign.

Now it hit home.

The character twisted rules created to protect into a cage for the vulnerable, and Kelly had been one of those vulnerable women. No wonder she flinched when he tried to touch her.

"You know what I think?" Pops asked as he stood up slowly and groaned. "I don't think it was a mistake that you ended up in my home."

Neither did Trevor.

"Here's a bit of advice from an old timer." He put his hand on Trevor's shoulder. "When I had my Nell, we didn't need anything but each other in the bedroom. That was more than enough. When you find the woman you're going to spend the rest of your life with, you don't need all that… stuff. You only need *her*."

MARK PUSHED OPEN Kelly's door and found it odd that the lights were off at this time of the day. Usually she was up. "Babe?"

"I'm here."

He went over to her bed and found her under the covers. "You sick?"

"Sick of people waking me up," she grumbled and sat up, her blonde hair a mess about her shoulders.

"Seriously, you do not have pretty bed head," he teased. "Are there rats in there?" He reached over as if to check and she swatted him away.

"Back off, jackass."

Mark laughed and was glad to see her smile. "Sooo? Why are you hibernating?"

"I'm an idiot with issues." Kelly crawled out of bed and went to her bathroom to brush her hair.

"More issues than National Geographic. I disagree about the idiot part, though." Mark leaned against the door jam.

"I totally freaked out in front of Trevor and he probably thinks I'm mentally unstable now."

"Well, you are." He laughed and Kelly threw her brush at him. "I'm teasing, jeez. What happened?"

"His latest script hits too close to home."

"It's about spousal abuse?"

"No, Mark. I mean it really hit home."

She didn't have to go further. Mark exhaled deeply and tried not to be overwhelmed with the emotions that accompanied the thoughts of Kelly's past—his past. "I'm sorry, babe." He pulled her into his arms. "Guess that's not the kind of role you want to see your celebrity crush play, huh?"

"Is that foolish? Because I feel so foolish for thinking he should care what I think. The man is so far beyond… well…me."

"No. I understand. It's not the type of movie people

like us enjoy. We've seen the bad side of that lifestyle and it's going to affect us differently. Kelly, you have to remember, not all women are going to react the same. Most women will pay two or three times to see Trevor Jacobs in that type of role. They'll get turned on by it."

Kelly dislodged from her best friend. "I know. But his character is a monster."

"Yeah, but that shit does well. People want more sex."

Kelly sighed. "Guess I just thought he was above all that."

Mark pushed hair out of her face. "People can't always live on the pedestals we set them on. You created whatever expectations you have of him based on characters in movies, Kelly. He's not any of those wonderful guys either. Why don't you try to get to know him for who he is? He might turn out to be a good guy in a different way."

"DAMN, MARK. YOU'VE been watching way too much Dr. Phil."

He slapped her ass and chuckled. "Bite me, I have brains. I'm not just a pretty face."

No one could ever call Mark ugly. He was gorgeous. His brown hair hung in silky sheets to his ears and his blue eyes always danced with mischief. A killer smile and gym-friendly body topped off the pretty package. It was a shame he was still single. Unfortunately, if there was one thing Mark didn't excel at, it was commitment.

She made sure her face didn't betray the fact she'd been crying. Then she and Mark went to find Trevor. He was on the veranda having evening cigars with Pops. Both men smiled at her and Trevor rose from his chair. "Can we talk?" He glanced at Mark. "Alone?"

Kelly nodded and retreated to one of the bedrooms. Before he could speak, she cut him off.

"I'm sorry. I never should have reacted so terribly. This is your life and your career and even though that movie might not appeal to me, it will to millions of other women. I'm a complete stranger to you. My opinion is null and void and you should do what you think is best for your career."

Trevor stared at her, silent.

"Now would be the time you should tell me 'apology accepted and you're right, your opinion doesn't matter. Thanks anyway.'"

"Kelly." His shoulders tensed up and he opened his mouth three times before he could speak. "Your opinion does matter. A lot. The bat shit crazy thing is, I can't figure out why."

"Gee, thanks." She huffed and crossed her arms over her chest.

"What I mean is, I've been criticized from day one. No matter what you do in Hollywood, someone, some-eff-ing-one is going to be against it. It's unavoidable. For years I've been able to ignore those people. They don't bother me, never have. But I really had to question why you getting so upset with me burned me up."

Kelly's head snapped up. What did he just say?

"You got so mad and my first reaction was to get defensive because no one gets mad at me anymore, at least not to my face. They usually kiss my ass. Then when you stormed off, I realized—" He looked her straight in the eyes. "You were being true and honest. I don't want you to be disappointed in me. Not as a fan and not as…a friend. I'm fresh out of ideas as to *why* except that I like you and I appreciate that you're honest and expressive and your grandfather is a funny old man who I respect. None of you have treated me like anything more than a normal person. It's nice. Pops scolded me. I haven't been put in my place like that in years.

I'm nearly thirty and he made me feel thirteen."

Kelly couldn't help it. She laughed. The way his eyes turned into those of a child made her almost feel sorry for him.

"It's not funny. I thought he was going to take me over his knee or something." Kelly's laughter made him crack a smile. "I couldn't beat up an old man, so that would have been an awkward moment." He rubbed the back of his neck.

Kelly had happy tears forming in her eyes. Trevor was every bit the decent, sweet guy she'd thought him to be. "Thank you for not kicking my Pop's ass. I appreciate that."

"Are we good? 'Cause I'd really like for us to be good."

Kelly nodded and when he opened his arms, she couldn't resist. The moment she breathed in his scent, she should have pulled away. It was now engrained in her brain. His cologne was magnificent, sandalwood and male musk.

God. Trevor Jacobs was hugging her, calling her his friend, telling her he liked her.

She definitely owed Mark a kidney.

Chapter Six

TREVOR NEVER SHOULD have held her. First mistake. Now he knew what her body felt like against his. The impression of her frame branded him. There was no way he was getting out of this house without feeling her again.

Second mistake. Allowing Mark to pick their movie. Pops, Kelly, and Mark had a tradition of watching movies together. They ordered pizza, drank soda and beer, ate popcorn, and made fun of whatever flick they chose.

And guess who they decided to make fun of tonight? Their new actor friend. His ass was toast. Yet, with this crew, he didn't mind so much.

"For tonight's viewing pleasure we have *Captured*, starring the talented Trevor Jacobs and the lovely Jenna McKeiver, who I would do in a heartbeat. Trevor, you lucky bastard," Mark said to the group.

"I'll give her your number."

Mark gave him a fist bump.

As the movie started, Pops and Mark took the two recliners on either side of a plush love seat. Kelly hesitated as they both realized at the same time they would be sitting together.

"You think we've treated you well thus far, just you

wait, Hollywood." She winked at him and his libido winked back.

Sure enough, they gave him hell, he and Jenna both. They threw popcorn at the television during the romance scenes, they degraded the special effects, and they even made fun of his stunts. Through it all, he laughed his ass off.

"Oh, come on," Kelly yelled as she threw popcorn at Jenna during a kissing scene. "He's playing you like a fiddle. Don't fall for that cheesy line. Stupid boys." The three men in the room threw popcorn at her. Her husky laugh was infectious and he found himself under her spell.

Did she know she was more beautiful than the actress on the screen? Did she even have a clue how much sweeter she was than Jenna?

"She sneezed on me during this scene," Trevor said.

Mark paused the movie. "*Yuck*."

"No joke. She was getting a cold and she actually sneezed in my face." Everyone cringed. "Yeah, I offered her a breath mint and she got offended."

"You. Did. Not." Mark rolled over laughing.

Trevor gave a sheepish shrug. "She didn't appreciate the gesture."

"How old is she?" Mark asked.

Trevor had to think about it. He didn't get too cozy with her during filming. "I don't know, honestly."

"She looks about twelve," Kelly said.

"I think you might have broken the law with that girl," Mark teased him.

"You know." Pops held up his hand. He had to have Italian heritage because neither he nor Kelly could speak without using hand gestures. "When I was a young man, the girls married around fifteen. Grandma Nell was only sixteen when I married her. Seventeen when your father was born, Kelly. This movie was supposed to be in that era. So that's about right."

"Thanks, Pops." Trevor raised his beer to him.

"But that girl still looks like she's twelve so that makes you one sick pup." Pops threw a handful of popcorn at him while Kelly and Mark cracked up laughing. Trevor nearly spit out his beer. God, they were too damned comical. That's where Kelly got her spunk. No wonder she was a handful. It was in her DNA.

About that time, one of the fight scenes of the movie came on. Trevor's character, an FBI agent, ran up the side of a wall and did a back flip to avoid the assailant.

Pops motioned to the screen. "Did you do all that?"

"I do all my stunts unless they are life threatening and the insurance company gets nervous."

"Do it. I want to see you run up a wall like that."

Trevor blanched. "Seriously?"

"You said you could. Prove it, pretty boy."

"Do it." Mark clapped; he was buzzed too.

"Boys are stupid." Kelly rolled her eyes and watched the screen.

Not one to pass up the opportunity to show off years of martial arts training, Trevor rose and emptied the contents of his pockets. He checked out the wall to the left of the room that had no pictures on it. Backing up as far as he could, he took off running, went two steps up the wall and used his legs to kick himself over into a back flip. He landed in a crouch and Pops nearly came out of his recliner. He threw his hands up in the air and yelled, "*Hey.*" and clapped.

"Ten," Kelly called from the couch.

"My turn." Pops stood up from his recliner.

"Sit down," Mark said laughed. "You'll lose your false teeth." Pops waved him off.

Feeling quite proud of himself, Trevor flopped down on the couch and joked about pulling an ass muscle.

When the movie was over, Pops excused himself to go to bed. Kelly walked him to his room. It provided Trevor the perfect opportunity to quiz Mark, especially since he was buzzed.

"So what's the deal with you and Kelly?"

"She's my best friend. What of it?" He took a swig of his beer.

"Just wondering. You two seem close."

"We are." Mark sobered up quick. He bent over and rested his hands on his knees. "What's on your brain, man?"

"She's cool, ya know?"

"Damn straight she is."

"And I'd like to get to know her better."

"Why?"

That was a pretty obvious answer, right? Trevor scoffed. "Why not?"

"If you're looking for a quick lay, look somewhere else. She's not up for grabs. You're leaving at some point."

"Mark, do you have any idea how talented a photographer she is? Pops showed me her portfolio today and—" He shook his head in disbelief. "She could be huge. She has untapped potential that the market would love."

"Trevor, let's get one thing straight real fast. Kelly is…" He searched the ceiling for the right words. "The best girlfriend I could never have. You understand what I'm saying? She's the greatest woman you will never have. Because the last asshole that had her ruined her. I'll be damned if I will let another man hurt her again. Be her friend, chitchat, like her all you want. For real though, keep your junk in your pants and away from her."

"Who the hell gave you the right to dictate who she's with?"

"She did. The night she called me because my brother beat and whipped her until she lost the baby in her belly."

All the blood drained from Trevor's head. The pizza and beer that had been so tasty mere moments ago roiled in his stomach.

"I'M BACK," KELLY said as she came back in the den. Pops was in his room and safely in bed. Too bad she wasn't tired. "Do you guys want to watch another movie? I rented some comedies—" She studied the two men. Mark's jaw was clenched and Trevor was an unhealthy shade of green. "What? What did I miss?"

Trevor stood and smoothed down his jeans. "I'm not used to eating like this and I'm afraid my stomach can't handle it. I think I'm going to take off for tonight."

"Are you okay? Do need me to get you—"

"No." He smiled at her, but his eyes were full of sadness. "I'll be fine. Good night, Kelly. Mark."

"Later, man." Mark saluted him with his beer bottle, then took a swig.

Kelly waited until she couldn't hear his footsteps in the hall and zeroed in on Mark. "What did you do?"

"Guy can't hold his beer. How's that my fault?"

"Cut the crap, Mark. You're a terrible liar. What did you do?"

Mark stood up to throw away his beer bottle. "Nothing, okay? He started asking questions about us and I let him know you weren't up for grabs."

"Us? Us as in being a couple? Explain. *Now.*"

"Listen, babe, the guy's interested. He's just not the type for you. He'll leave and then what? You think he's going to carry on a long distance relationship with you when he could have any—" Mark stopped and swallowed whatever words he was about to say.

Kelly crossed her arms over her chest and narrowed her eyes. "When he could have any *what*, Mark?"

He averted his eyes. "I don't want to finish that sentence."

"No, you don't and I don't want to finish this conversation. You can't drive home, but I suggest you pick a room far away from my studio." She turned to leave, but Mark caught her arm.

"Come on, Kelly, I'm only looking out for you. I don't want this guy to think you're some floozy he can bag-n-tag. You deserve better."

"*I* will be the judge of who and what I deserve and want, thank you very much."

Kelly stormed out of the room. She needed to straighten things out with Trevor. The last thing she needed was more miscommunication on that front. Her fist stopped mid-air before she knocked on the door.

What exactly was she going to say? *"I don't know what Mark told you, but you can bag-n-tag me any day of the week and twice on Sundays."*

"Damn it." She took off down the hall away from his room.

"Kelly?" Trevor stuck his head out the door.

Damn these old houses with their creaky floors. She bit her lip and turned. "Sorry, I was just going to check on you, but then I thought if you were having stomach problems you might want to be left alone." *Yeah, because that sounds so much better than option A.*

He nodded, but couldn't meet her eyes. "Good night."

She paced the floor of her studio. What was wrong with her? Everything was so messed up in her head right now. Nothing made sense. Trevor had come to town and blown her brainpower to smithereens. She looked at her bed, her *sexy* bed.

Sleep would help. Sleep always helped. Tomorrow she would wake up with a clear head and she could focus on important things like…like…things that were important.

With teeth brushed, face washed, and her favorite pajamas slinking over her skin, Kelly climbed into bed and relaxed into the covers. *Perfection.*

Not even the bed made her forget the warmth of Trevor's delectable body or the sadness in his eyes when he looked at her.

Damn it.

Chapter Seven

"KELLY?"

Her name was being whispered from far off and she didn't want to respond. If it was Mark waking her up at three in the morning again, so help her, she was going to make good on that threat against his junk.

"Kelly?"

Oh hell. Not Mark.

"Are you awake?"

"I am now, thanks for nothing. What do you want, Trevor?" Kelly's heart fluttered. Why was he in her room?

"Mark was right; you really aren't a nice person in the middle of the night."

"Then I suggest leaving the beast alone. G'night." She rolled back over and cuddled up to her pillow. Her mattress dipped. Oh. Dear. God.

Trevor was sitting on the edge. Why was he in her room? Didn't he have any respect for personal space? She tried to pace her breathing.

"I can't sleep. If I don't talk to you, I'll never be able to shut my eyes."

Kelly muttered some rather blue words and sat up in bed. "Talk," she grumbled.

"I'm not going to do the film."

"What film?" Kelly asked as her body swayed, trying to find the comfort of her pillows again.

"Do I need to make coffee? I really need you to concentrate. This is all your fault and I want to talk to you about it."

Kelly sighed, her brain refusing wake up. "How about we make a trade? You come lay down, I lay down, and we can talk in the morning. I promise you will sleep in this bed. It's magic." Her last words were muffled by a yawn. She patted the space next to her. "Come on, Hollywood. We can both need to catch some z's."

"We can talk about this tomorrow, right? You promise?"

"Yes, just sleep. Then talk. Wait, first coffee, then talk."

She vaguely registered him laughing and settling in the bed beside her. "You realize this is a bad idea, sleeping together."

"I'll try to keep my hands to myself," she joked and smiled to herself.

"And if I don't?"

"Hollywood, I'm one of those women that doesn't socialize at this hour. So don't touch me with anything you want back. Got it?"

"Yep, Mark was right. Evil." He whispered that last word and she covered her giggle.

KELLY SNUGGLED INTO the pillows, reluctant to acknowledge the sunshine coming through her windows. The sweet heavenly smell of coffee tickled her nose. As she blinked open her eyes, she thought she must still be dreaming.

Trevor stood, shirtless in flannel pants sipping coffee as he looked out the tall arched windows. She drank in the sight of him. The reality of his good looks and sculpted body were far better than any movie or picture she had ever seen.

Had he actually slept in *her* bed last night? Shirtless? Holy crap. She had to be the stupidest woman on the planet to sleep through that.

"Would it be weird for me to admit that I am totally crushing on you right now?" She smiled and hugged her pillow. His smile spread slowly across his face as he padded barefoot to her bed.

"Would it be any weirder than admitting last night was the first time I have literally slept with a woman?"

Oh, God. She could not allow herself to follow that train of thought. Time to derail. "Slept with a lot of men, though, huh?"

Trevor choked on his coffee. "That's not what I meant, smartass."

Kelly smiled until she remembered what Mark said about her ugly bed head. She ran her hands over her blonde hair in hopes it wasn't too bad.

"Coffee?" He handed her the mug and she inhaled the steamy warmth of it.

"Thank you." For a time, they sat and sipped in comfortable silence.

Trevor slid up onto the bed and rested his back on the headboard, his posture mirroring hers.

"Can I ask you something?" he asked softly.

No. "Sure."

"Are you in love with Mark?"

"Wow, you know how to start the morning off awkward, don't ya?"

"I'd like to know."

"No, I don't love Mark in a romantic way. It wouldn't work between us because of our history and his tendency to

49

flee from commitment like it's the plague."

"Because he was your brother-in-law?"

Kelly swore under her breath and clenched her jaw. *Damn Mark.* "What did he tell you?"

"Enough to know why you reacted so negatively to the screenplay."

"I told you, this isn't about me. You have to do what's best for your career." Kelly needed room to think. She carefully scooted out of bed, but Trevor followed. "It's none of my concern."

"What if I want it to be your concern?"

She froze at his words and pivoted on one heel. "That's ridiculous. You don't know me. I don't know you."

"You've got to give me something here, Kelly." He sighed, his hands going to his trim hips and drawing her eyes to the light dusting of hair that disappeared under the flannel.

"I might need more coffee because I don't know what you're talking about." Kelly avoided looking at him by heading in the opposite direction. She knew damned well what he was talking about. She just didn't want to talk about it.

"Are you attracted to me at all?" Trevor asked with a laugh. "Because I can usually tell when a woman is and you haven't given off any of the signs. I know there's something there, yet we shared a bed for half the night and you didn't so much as cuddle."

Kelly rounded on him and put her hands on her hips before she realized she wasn't wearing a bra, then she crossed her arms over her chest. "You're a famous movie star, Trevor. Half the world is attracted to you. So ask yourself honestly." She shrugged and looked away again. "Does it actually matter if I am or not?"

"Of course it does." He threw up his hands.

"It might now, Trevor. In this moment when you're

secluded from the world and your lifestyle and your day-to-day, it might matter. But I assure you, once you go…" She ran her hands through her hair. The very thought of him leaving hurt her heart and it was not a welcome feeling. "You'll never think of me again."

"I highly doubt that."

Kelly needed to sit somewhere that didn't have a bed. "I've seen the girls you date, Trevor. I don't fit that mold."

"Those girls have the brain capacity of bowling pins. They're props, Kelly."

"That makes it so much better, thanks for sharing." Kelly rolled her eyes.

"You have to understand what I mean. I didn't want relationships with them."

"Only sex?"

"No. God, no. I mean, I'm no virgin, but not all of them were worth the time." He shook his head wildly at the idea and that made her feel a bit better. "First off, you shouldn't believe what you read in the tabloids or what TMZ reports. Second, those women were simply seat fillers, women that look good on your arm as you walk down the red carpet."

"What am I? Another filler? A babysitter until you return to the Hollywood hills?"

"Damn woman, your Pops was right. You have this unbreakable wall around you. Do you ever let anyone in?"

Kelly's eyes filled with moisture until she had to blink it away. "He said that?" she whispered.

"Yeah. Mark too. At least he's inside the wall looking out." Trevor sat on the arm of a chair and ran his hands down his face.

Kelly didn't want to be the person he was talking about, even if she did have just cause. Knowing she had to give him something, any piece of herself before he turned away, she took a deep breath and exhaled through her mouth. Tears pricked her eyes.

"I was married to Mark's brother. That's why he's on the inside."

Trevor raised his head, his eyes fastened on hers.

"It was the age old high school sweethearts crap. He was on the football team, I was a cheerleader, the whole cliché. We had been married about two years when he comes home from a night out with his buddies and says that we should spice up our love life. We were in a sexual rut, I'll admit. The honeymoon was over and between his job and my college classes, we were growing distant. Not a good sign two years in." Kelly traced the rim of her coffee cup. She would have given anything to never talk about this again. Trevor was worth the sacrifice.

"He had a friend that tried some of that stuff with his wife. Role playing, light bondage. Nothing that anyone would ever call harmful, even me. Their marriage did well and they kept the focus on pleasing each other. I think when this kind of thing came about, that was the original intention." She met his eyes. "But it doesn't always turn out so well. He suggested we try it and at that point I was willing to do just about anything to make him happy. I loved him so much and I never thought twice." Even now, remembering the good times of her marriage made her smile. Craig was a lot like Mark: funny, smart, handsome—so very handsome. Unfortunately, his smiles and charisma hid something ugly underneath.

"We started out small, toys or gags, but after a while he got bored with that and he would come up with something more aggressive. It was kind of fun at first. It felt wrong enough to make it exciting, but not enough to bother me. It's just…" Kelly bit her bottom lip to keep from crying. "… addictions like that have a tendency to snowball. Before you know it, you're barreling downhill and you can't stop the momentum. It happens so gradually that you never realize how far you've slipped until one day you don't recognize your own reflection. That's what happened to Craig. No one saw that side of him except me. No one else knew that our love life had become his sick game. I played because he was my husband, but never came out the winner." A lump formed in her throat.

Trevor hadn't moved a muscle. He stared at her, his face etched in stone. There was no telling what he was thinking.

"When I found out I was pregnant, I was so happy. The thought of being a mom was scary, but I wanted that baby from the moment I found out. I knew it was what Craig and I needed. He wanted to get deeper into the sexual games, but I thought if he knew he was going to be a father, it might snap him out of it. Most men do that, right? They settle down after they become fathers." Kelly's body shook. She wrapped her arms around herself as if to keep her from physically falling apart.

"You don't have to do this," Trevor whispered. "I can fill in the blanks."

There was no stopping a moving train. Now that she'd started, she couldn't stop. Tears fell down her cheeks. "He thought I was lying. I planned this romantic evening and made his favorite dinner. I called him at work to let him know I had a special night planned. Craig assumed I was taking him up on his offer. He came home in such a good mood. We had dinner, we danced in the living room, he told me how much he loved me and that he was so glad we could live like this together. I was his dream girl. Those were his words." She shook her head and wiped her eyes. "I had no idea. I had no idea that I could go from being his dream to being his nightmare so quickly. When I told him I was pregnant and we couldn't do those things anymore, he said I was holding back on him. He couldn't stand the thought of me being pregnant. How would I look beautiful if I was fat? How would he be able to get off if all he saw was my bloated belly and stretch marks?"

"Stop." Trevor stood up and pulled Kelly into his arms. "You don't have to say anything else. You don't have to relive this." He held her so tight she could feel the way his heart pounded. His lips went to her ear. "I'm so sorry, Kelly. I'm sorry I dredged up such ugliness back into your life. I won't do the film. I'll call my agent."

SHE PULLED BACK to look into his eyes. "You don't have to do that for me."

"Of course I do. How could I ever look in the mirror if I did a movie that glorified this behavior knowing what I know now? You can't possibly be the only woman out there that's suffered."

She reached up and touched his cheek, her heart softening when he leaned in to her palm. "You have more influence than you know, Trevor. Do you comprehend what turning this role down might do to you? People are going to want to know why. I'm sure there's a line of actors willing to play this part."

"Then let them." His voice was stern, unwavering. He held her longer, tighter. Kelly cradled her head under his chin and inhaled his scent until she could open her eyes and not see Craig's face.

Trevor stroked her arms until she was ready to face him again. "I want to be the type of man women like you would be a fan of."

"Women like me?" Kelly arched a brow, nearly giddy at his words. When he smiled, all the final shadows of her past dissipated.

He cupped her cheek. "Especially you. Only you."

As his face inched towards hers, Kelly's heart nearly jumped out of her chest. He was going to kiss her. *Oh God,* he was going to kiss—her cheek? *What the hell?*

"If I kiss you right now, when you're crying and upset, you might look back and think I was taking advantage of the situation. That's not the way I want this to be." He pulled back and made sure he had her full attention.

Uneasy with the serious connotation of his words, she couldn't help but try to back the train up. "Does that mean we can't have fun, meaningless sex? Because I was rather looking forward to that eventually."

"I have a feeling the sex will never be meaningless between us."

The way he stared made her temperature rise.

"I'm sure that's what you tell all the ladies," Kelly teased as she unfolded from his grasp. She picked up her coffee cup. "I've seen those sex scenes in your movies. You can't tell me there wasn't some behind the scenes action going on."

The guilty look on his face was her answer and wasn't *that* just the cool down she needed?

Chapter Eight

TREVOR ALLOWED HER to change the subject. The progression of their relationship was going to scare her and he accepted that she would feel the need to build up her defenses again. He went along with her jokes, but deep down, he was still very much aware of the desire that simmered between them.

"Only once," he confessed. "You might not believe this, but I am a trained actor. So I can fake it."

"I'll keep that in mind, but I still don't believe it. There's no way you can be as intimate as you were with that blonde chick in *Kills for Thrills*. That was one step away from being X-rated."

Boy, had she pegged it. He swallowed the tennis ball in his throat and scratched his neck, a nervous habit. "You're way too perceptive at times, Kelly."

Her mouth fell open. "Her? She's the one?"

"We dated for a while, before and after that movie. Things were getting serious until she began shooting another film and it ended badly."

"I remember that. It was all over the rags. How she broke your heart and cheated several times." She gave him the pouty puppy dog face. "How did you ever recover?"

"I'm heartbroken to this day, can't you tell?" He liked the way she teased him, liked the way she could take just as much as she gave.

Kelly chuckled as she went to her computer and sat down. "Would you like to see the shots from yesterday?"

Her photography talent intrigued him. These shots didn't disappoint. The couple was going to flip when they saw how Kelly captured the dynamic of their interactions. The woman's smiles, the guy's adoring gaze. It gave him a prickling sensation in his chest. Would Kelly ever smile at him with that level of affection in her eyes?

"Trevor?"

"Huh?" He snapped back to attention.

"I said, do you want to take a walk with me so I can get some nature shots?" She tilted her head at him. "Are you okay?"

"Yeah, I'm simply blown away by your skills. You have a gift."

A stage spotlight didn't shine as bright as the grin she gave him. "Thanks."

One thing he really appreciated about Kelly was her ability to treat him as she would any other person in her life. He even liked it when she took a phone call and held up a finger to shush him. It struck him as insane. He always hated the way his entourage revolved around him. How many times had he wanted to stop and shout, *"Go get your own damn lives!"*?

Yet, here was Kelly, biting her bottom lip. "Friday night? As in tomorrow night?" She glanced over at him. "I kind of have prior commitments, Stacy."

Trevor shook his head and waved a hand at her. He didn't want her life to be placed on hold for him.

"Let me see what I can do and then I'll call you back, okay? Yeah, I know dancing sounds great and we haven't done it in a while. God knows I could use a drink too."

He could hear the laughter and chatting from the woman on the other end. Judging by Kelly's return giggles, they were close friends. She hung up and turned back to him. "Would that be really rude of me to go have drinks with my friends when you're here?"

"Not at all. You're not supposed to babysit me, Kelly. Besides, maybe Pops would like to hang out. Does he watch any sports or just those westerns?"

"Pops? You're volunteering to spend an evening with my grandfather?" Skepticism colored her face.

"You have a life, Kelly. Don't worry about me. Besides, I really do like your grandfather."

A debate waged in her head. He could practically hear the wheels turning. *Should she go? Should she stay?*

"I guess I'll confirm with Stacy then. Too bad you couldn't come along. I know my friends would peg you the moment they saw you."

"More adoring fans?" He popped his collar and tried to look smug.

Kelly raised her camera and clicked a picture of him posing. "I'll make sure to let them know you're actually a pompous ass." She slapped his arm as she went by.

Man, she was getting to him good.

They meandered through the woods for another hour. All the while, she snapped pictures. He even convinced her to take one of them together. She made some excuse about evidence of his time there. He called her a chicken and that was all it took to change her stubborn mind. Evidence was exactly what he wanted and needed. It would always remind him of his time with her. He snapped a couple pictures of her alone before she reclaimed the camera.

Kelly asked him questions about himself that made him think. Surprising, since he'd been interviewed more times that he'd care to recall. The thing was, she didn't ask fan questions. What was his favorite movie, what was his favorite song, what did he prefer to eat, boxers or briefs? She had much deeper interests.

How did he handle the fact that so many people wanted things from him? He tried to focus on the people he cared about and keeping the majority of his fans entertained. How did he ever know who was his true friend versus a fame hunter? That was easy. He could tell within the first meeting.

"What did you think of me?" she asked.

"I thought you were a pain in the ass cause you believed that whole drugs and hooker story."

Kelly laughed and stepped over a fallen tree. He watched the way her jeans stretched over her legs and backside. "No, that's not entirely true. I thought you were a *beautiful* pain in the ass cause you believed that whole drugs and hooker story."

When she looked over her shoulder, her blonde hair caught a breeze and lifted. "Beautiful? At four in the morning? You're full of crap."

"That was the other thing that made me trust you. You were a total brat where most women fawn or flirt or giggle like idiots."

He nearly lost his footing when she turned and gave him a look of pure seduction, her lips pouty and her eyes hooded. "What's the matter, big boy?" She ran a hand over his chest and even though she was playing him, he so wanted to indulge in this game. "Didn't get that big ego stroked?" Those lips were temptation.

To shock the hell out of her, he bent down and took that pouty bottom lip between his teeth and kissed her. Her gasp was all the proof of success he needed. When he pulled back, she was wide-eyed and her mouth was a glistening pink color. "Be careful, Kelly, or I'll have you stroking more than my ego." He grinned and left her standing there. "Come on, like you didn't see that coming," he called over his shoulder.

"I don't think I did."

The awe in her voice made him smile. He was getting to her after all.

When they reached a fantastic lookout point, Trevor sat down on a log that had been placed there for just that reason. "Incredible."

"This was my favorite place to come when I was a kid." Kelly sat down beside him and crossed her arms over her knees.

"You said your parents were gone. What does that mean?" He straddled the log so he could see her better.

"They died in a freak accident when I was a baby. I never really knew them. Pops and Grandma Nell raised me."

"I'm sorry."

She brushed off his sympathy. "A person can't really be angry at a bridge collapsing. It's not as if they were murdered or anything. People die; it's a fact of life. It's hard to mourn something you never had. I had a great childhood, though. Grandma Nell and Pops were the best parents a kid could ask for. They were good about keeping my parent's memories alive. We have picture albums and home movies. My grandparents helped me have peace about it."

"My mom died when I was thirteen."

"I didn't know that. I'm sorry. That's totally different. You had thirteen years to love her."

"Yeah, I definitely know what I lost. Especially when my dad remarried. You know those evil step-monsters in the movies? That's not based on pure fiction."

"Oh boy. Tell me about her." Kelly listened as he spoke first of his mother and then of his father's evil bride. The woman had made his childhood hell and didn't want to have anything to do with him until he'd landed his first major role.

"Suddenly she was the adoring mother. I wanted to punch her." He laughed.

"My uncle married one of those. Pops calls her the money-grubbing harlot—to her face."

"To her face?" Trevor could see the old man doing it too.

"They don't come around much."

He threw his head back, laughing. God, he loved that man. What he would give to have someone like that in his life.

As if conjured by the mention of his name, they heard Pops yelling from further down the hillside. "Kelly? You out there?"

She hopped to her feet and went to the edge of the overlook. He wanted to tell her to be careful, but didn't figure it would settle well. They were close to the estate, looking down into the back gardens. Kelly waved her arms and called to Pops.

He covered his eyes and looked upward. "Lunch!"

"Oh my God." Kelly checked her watch. "We've been gone for three hours. I have a shoot at one. We're going to have to take the shortcut back."

Before he could question her, she was securing her camera strap around her back and stepping off the overlook.

"Kelly!"

"Come on stunt man, don't be a chicken. Grab a rope."

That was when he saw her holding on to her own rope and using it to guide her down the side of the steep hill. "You scared the crap out of me."

"Wimp," she called from much lower.

So help him, he was never going to be the same after spending time with her.

Chapter Nine

THEY INHALED LUNCH. Kelly had to clean and set up for this afternoon's shoot. An older woman wanted a portrait done with her Pomeranian, Princess. She shivered at the thought of that five-pound ball of terror.

A quick shower was necessary after her morning hike. Trevor said he could hang with Pops again, which was fine with her. She still had about thirty minutes until one, so she could afford to slow down and take a breather.

She came out of her bathroom wearing nothing but the towel she was drying her hair with as cover. The iPod blared her favorite music and she danced along to the music. Her feet were in the middle of a fancy jig, her hips circling with the rhythm.

"Wow."

"SHIT," Kelly screamed.

Trevor sat on her bed with a bag of popcorn in his hands.

"What the hell are you doing in here?" She scrambled to cover her most vital parts with her towel. Those parts and everything in between went hot with a blush.

"I was going to hide in here and watch you do your photo shoot, but this is a much better show." He popped a kernel in his mouth and smiled like the Cheshire cat, one brow raised in obvious male appreciation. "You have some moves, gorgeous."

"You can't stay in here. I'm *naked* for Christ's sake."

"Oh, I can see that. Perfect ten by the way." He started laughing. The punk was enjoying himself way too much. She, on the other hand, wanted to crawl in a hole.

Kelly's phone rang and she was mortified that she had to go to her nightstand to answer it. For a moment, she considered letting it to go voicemail just so she could stay across the room. Trevor watched every move and he had much more than a peep show on his mind. The ringing stopped and started back up again. She nearly stomped her foot before walking over to the nightstand and picking it up.

"Hello?" Kelly answered as she dove under her sheets and yanked them to her chin.

Trevor tried to pull the sheet until she slapped him on the head.

"Kelly, this is Mrs. Ragland. I hate to do this on such short notice, but I need to cancel. Something is wrong with my little Princess and we're taking her to the vet. Perhaps we can reschedule when she's better?"

"Absolutely, Mrs. Ragland, and I hope your dog is all right. I'll talk to you soon."

She didn't mean to hang up so abruptly, but Trevor had stretched out on the bed.

"Canceled?"

"Yes, my photo shoot and your peepshow," she bit out. "Now if you don't mind, I would like to get dressed please."

He shook his head and crinkled his nose. His grin never faltered.

"Fine." Kelly threw her legs over the side of the bed to stand up, but Trevor grabbed the towel and she was left completely exposed.

"That worked out better than I planned." He chuckled as her face burned. When she reached for the sheet, he slapped her hand. "Nope."

Damn it to hell.

Wet hair dripped down her back and made her cold, but Trevor wouldn't let her near the bed to cover up. Add his laughter and sexy mischievous smile to the mix and realized what a picture they made. The way his eyes traveled up and down the length of her body caused her breasts to tighten. She squeezed her thighs together and hoped he didn't notice.

Being the defiant woman she was, Kelly took a deep breath and squared her shoulders, put her hands on her hitched hip, and stared him down. "All right, Hollywood. You win. You've got me naked, now what they hell do you plan on doing?"

Trevor threw the popcorn bag over his head and reached for her. He was quick and Kelly didn't have time to fight. Instead, she giggled and kicked as he hauled her onto the bed and blanketed her with his body. Popcorn was all over her bed and floor. Not that it mattered. She tried to fight him, but was laughing too hard.

"Kiss me," he commanded, his lips centimeters from hers.

"Bite me."

"Even better." Trevor buried his face in the curve of her neck and bit down lightly, just enough to have her squirming. He kissed the stinging flesh and the area around it. Kelly couldn't control the moan that escaped. Her neck was ultra-sensitive.

"You like that?" he whispered.

"You went straight for my weakness. That's not fair."

"Who said anything about playing fair?"

Kelly chuckled and maneuvered her hips so she rubbed against the strained zipper of his jeans. Trevor sucked in a breath and reached down to cup her bottom with one hand.

"What's your game then, Trevor? What are you trying

to start?"

"I would think that was obvious. Maybe I should try another tactic." He dipped his head to her breast and Kelly saw stars. She arched against him and scrambled to take his shirt off. Once that was done, she gloried in the skin-to-skin contact. She ran her hands over his ripped chest and received a reward.

Trevor groaned and lifted his head. "Now who's not playing fair?"

Kelly lifted her head and slid her tongue over his skin. His curses painted the room blue.

"Now you've done it." He spanked her rear and sat up to remove his jeans. Kelly watched with rapt interest.

The practical person inside rose to the surface. They barely knew each other. "Trevor, I don't know if we should—"

"Don't. Don't try to say this isn't right." He came back to lie beside her and pushed the hair off her shoulder. "Out of everything and everyone in my life right now, you're the only thing that seems real to me."

"You still seem unreal to me. I keep getting deeper and deeper into this fantasy and I'm worried about what happens to me when it ends."

Trevor sighed and kissed her shoulder. "I can't make too many promises, but I can say this. Just because I get on a plane doesn't mean this ends. I want to give us a try."

Kelly's heart lurched. "You do? I'm not exactly the Hollywood red carpet type."

"I think that's what I love the most. I need that. I need you, Kelly."

"For how long?" Kelly sighed and put her head back on the pillows. In her mind, there was no way she walked away from this whole. That was more sobering than a cold shower.

"Okay." Trevor covered her body with the sheet and

settled in beside her, his head propped up on his elbow. "Let's get all this out there. What's on your mind, baby?"

She looked into his brown eyes. It was much different than looking at the poster she hid behind her bed. These eyes were warm and intense and focused solely on her. These eyes had the potential to rip her heart out.

"I'm crazy about you. But I don't know if it's the you I've seen on television or the man in the bed with me."

Trevor blew out a ragged breath and rolled over on his back.

"I want to believe it's the man in the bed with me. After lusting over you for years, there's no guarantee. I'm sorry, I can't imagine how insulting that must be for you."

"I'm not insulted." He rubbed his eyes and then looked at her. "I'm glad you're honest. Most women want to go to bed with the man on the screen. They don't give a damn about the real person."

"But I do." Kelly had to touch him, had to connect with him. As she rolled over and threw her leg over his waist, he turned to her and smiled. "That's why I put on the brakes. You should know that I understand the difference."

"I know you do. That's what makes you so irresistible."

"I don't want you to ever doubt me. I would rather you walk out that door and never see you again than to make love as you wonder what I'm really after. Yeah, I like the guy in the movies. He's been my favorite actor for a few years now. I've come to respect and care for the guy I picked up at the airport though."

Trevor smiled up at her and her heart melted. "I'm pretty crazy about you too." Wrapping Kelly in his arms, he buried his head in her neck and drew in a deep breath. "I'm not stupid enough to let you go. Think you can learn to live with that?"

"Yeah. Yeah, I can." Kelly gave in. She didn't want to hold back anymore. If there was one man worth risking her heart for, it was Trevor. Sure, up until yesterday he was a fantasy, someone untouchable. But as their bodies joined in a passionate dance, she was thankful for the reality.

Trevor mastered her body like a musician masters their instrument, slowly tuning her up then taking her to highs she'd never experienced. Their rhythm ranged from a smooth and gentle rocking ballad to a grand crescendo of bodies melting together with desperate need. It had been so long, too long, since she'd felt the intimate touch of a man. This particular man was trying to make her lose her mind. Not an inch of his toned flesh went unexplored. If this was to be the memory she kept of Trevor, it was going to last her the rest of her life. After being with him, she couldn't imagine it got any better. No one else could ever measure up.

TREVOR GROANED IN release. He reveled in the climax as he made love to Kelly. God, she was incredible. Her body had been so receptive and she gave as much as she received. Even now, she placed sweet kisses on his chest. He could still feel the spasms of her body around him.

"Amazing," he panted. "Absolutely…amazing." There was a vast difference in the sex he'd had before and the connection he'd just made with Kelly. *This* was what making love was really about. Pops was one hundred percent correct; all a man needs is to truly connect with the woman he's with.

"I second that." Kelly rolled off his body and cuddled up next to him. "This is probably a bad time to bring this up, but you should know I can't get pregnant."

Pregnant. Oh hell.

He'd never even stopped to consider using a condom with her. Odd, since it was usually his first priority with other women. He kissed her head. "Are you sure about that, baby?" He didn't want to call her a liar, but it wasn't the first time he'd heard that line. "No offense, but I've had a girl use that line on me before."

It was a huge scandal. One of his ex-girlfriends popped up pregnant, claiming it was his kid. DNA testing had to be done even though Trevor claimed she was lying all along. It made a guy double check.

"I remember." She snuggled deeper into his side. "When I had my miscarriage, the doctors said I had too much internal damage to carry a child."

The ache in her voice made him want to shoot that sick bastard between the eyes. "I'm sorry, Kelly." He rolled over on top of her and looked into her eyes. "I didn't even think about using protection."

"Luckily you didn't need it," she joked, but it was a bandage covering a deep loss.

"What ever happened to him?"

"He's locked up, for now. Once the hospital figured out what happened, they had no choice but to get the law involved. He didn't want to settle out of court because he tried to claim he had no knowledge of the baby and that the beatings were part of our consensual sexual experience. There was a trial. It was awful. I've never been more humiliated in my life. For months I couldn't even go to the grocery store without someone stopping me to talk about it."

"Were they rude to you?"

"Well, I did have a guy tell me that losing my baby was a punishment for my sinful perversions."

Trevor's jaw dropped. "Are you kidding me?"

"He didn't last long around here. Turns out his own sinful lifestyle caught up with him—and the school secretary he was screwing. Her husband was a concrete contractor. I swear one day they are going to find that guy's body in the foundation of one of these houses around here." She shivered. "Everyone else just wanted to offer support or get the gossip. Craig's family was pretty well known. It was front page news."

"I'm sorry, baby." Trevor kissed her gently. He wanted nothing more than to take those memories and experiences away from her, but they molded her into the strong woman she was. The woman he was falling for.

"Can I show you something?"

Trevor let her up and waited while she retrieved her laptop. She came back to sit up in bed next to him. He liked the domestic intimacy of it. They were simply a normal couple sitting in bed together, talking.

She brought up the Internet and typed in a website he knew well. "When you took that trip to South Africa a couple years ago, I started following the organization you sponsored."

"You did?" He sat up, delighted that the trip had affected someone. It had been on a couple entertainment shows and he had articles in a few magazines, but they'd focused on him, not the children he'd gone to help. "That trip changed my life."

Kelly smiled up at him. "I could tell when you went on the Larry Quinton show that it really clicked for you." She blushed. "For me, it was the best interview you've ever done."

He could no more resist the urge to kiss her than he could resist the urge to breathe. She kissed him back with the same fervor that made his blood run fast.

"If you keep kissing me, I won't be able to talk and I've never shared this with anyone."

Trevor pulled back, a single brow raised. "Not even Mark?"

Her suppressed grin and sexy blush pushed him further over the abyss. "No, not even Mark." Kelly typed again on the laptop and brought up the South African organization that brought food and medical supplies to children. "After some digging, I discovered that they have an adoption agency who partners with an agency here in the States. I don't meet their requirements yet because I'm not married. They're big on a two-parent household. I've been sending donations ever since." Kelly didn't look at him for a moment. "I hope one day I can adopt from them."

He couldn't speak. He was floored. Not only was she donating to a charity that was special to him, one day she would adopt a child from that organization. "It's official," he said softly.

"What?"

"You're the most amazing woman in the world." Trevor moved the laptop to the bedside table and cradled Kelly in his arms. Her giving heart humbled him. "Why couldn't I have met you years ago?"

"Well you've met me now, Hollywood." Her hands roamed his naked chest and up to his hair. "And I'm damn happy about it."

"Me, too. I don't know how the hell I'm supposed to go back to my daily life without you. I don't guess you're interested in coming with me?"

Kelly gasped and her eyes widened. "Me? In Hollywood?" She shook her head and laughed. "No, Trevor. I would never be able to live like that."

"Why not? After a while it becomes normal."

"Yes, but," she said with a sigh and kissed his lips, "you thrive in the spotlight. It would shrivel me up like a raisin."

Trevor's chest ached at the thought of leaving her. The pain spread over his body, making it hard to think about anything else. "I want us to be together."

"We are, right now. Can we focus on that instead of borrowing tomorrow's troubles?"

He nodded, not trusting his voice to be steady. This issue would have to be addressed at some point in the near future. Hiding out in the mountains wasn't a long-term plan. Eventually he had to get back to California. But for today, he obliged Kelly and focused on loving her to the fullest.

"Put your legs around me," he said against her lips. As she slipped her tongue in his mouth, he buried himself in her luscious body. They spent the entire afternoon in bed, loving, talking, and discovering the various layers of each other. As many people as he'd met in his public life, none of them interested and intrigued him like Kelly. Their conversation went on for hours, only pausing long enough for a kiss or a touch. Seeing her melt and come undone in his hands quickly became his addiction. She filled a void in his life. How had he lived this long and not realized what he was missing? How could any man abuse a woman so funny and wonderful? If Kelly was his wife, he'd consider himself the luckiest man to walk the earth.

Chapter Ten

KELLY COULDN'T BELIEVE how quickly the next few days passed. She had no choice but to continue on with her normal routine. She went out dancing with her girlfriends and had photo shoots both on the house grounds and offsite. Each night she sat around the table with Pops, Trevor, and occasionally Mark for dinner.

What surprised her most was how easily Trevor assimilated into her daily activities. He was there to offer his opinions when she edited photos, he helped with dishes, and he even vacuumed the first floor living room when she rushed to get ready for a consultation. Each night they went to bed together and made love until they exhausted themselves.

It was so easy to get caught up in his affections. He voiced his feelings easier than she ever could. That must have come from his training as an actor. He'd told her how he prepared for a role by identifying the emotional needs and internal motivations of his characters.

It wasn't as easy for her. There were times when she could read the expectation in his face, but she couldn't say the right words. After locking up her emotions tight for so many years, it was a challenge to turn them loose now.

What got to her were the moments she saw Trevor and

Pops together. They worked in the yard, fixed various things around the house, and often sat out on the back deck with cigars. Trevor didn't share much of what they spoke about, but he did say how her grandfather was an inspiration and how he felt lucky to hear his words of wisdom. Of course, Kelly feared it wouldn't be her heart alone that would break in the end. Pops didn't get close to many people, but he'd poured out his advice and stories on Trevor like he was his long lost son. Maybe it was good for them both.

Trevor let his facial hair grow out, so after a couple weeks he was woolly, but not too recognizable. They made a trip to the grocery store together and went to the movies a few times, even hit a club and went dancing. Trevor was a toucher. He insisted on holding her hand or guiding her by resting his palm against the small of her back. When she thought about it, she realized his hands were always on her in some way. A touch of the cheek, playing with her hair, rubbing her shoulders, holding her hand. She wished more than anything to be as free with her physical affections, yet she held back.

Whether he wanted to think about it or not, he couldn't stay forever. No matter how many times he offered, she wouldn't go back with him. She couldn't. A small voice in the back of her abused mind feared all of this was an act. Trevor was paid millions of dollars to pretend to be in love with his co-stars all the time. Surely some of his actions were a result of that ability to fake love.

That fear didn't stop her from going to bed with him every night. She loved the way he ravished her body as if she were the most exotic woman on the planet. The women on television were thinner than she was, taller, better dressed and groomed. Trevor never compared her to them. That respect alone was worth every night she gave him.

Waking up to him was a gift too. He rose early and would work out while she slept in. Or pretended to. Seeing

Trevor work up a sweat had to be the biggest turn on of her life. Helping him wash the sweat off sated that hunger.

Letting him go was going to be so damned hard. Her chest ached each time she thought of it. But after three weeks of the famous Trevor Jacobs being MIA, the media was beginning to buzz. Talk show hosts were making jokes about it in their monologues. The tabloids were reporting him missing due to everything from death by overdose to rehab to running from the law. If he didn't surface soon, they would hunt him down like rabid wolves.

Kelly kept that at the forefront of her mind. He didn't belong to her. He never really could. They might share a bed, but sharing a life was impossible. She kept the wall around her heart strong. It would make the separation easier—she hoped.

AS THE SUN set on his third full week with Kelly, dread bubbled up in Trevor's gut. Tomorrow he had to check in with his people. Once he did, they would be on a deadline.

Jessica, his agent, would want to know exactly when he would be back and when they could start filming. No doubt the studio was pissed already.

God, he didn't want to leave. He didn't know if he could.

He walked out of the bathroom and saw her in skimpy purple silk against the white bedding. The finest work of art, even as she checked her email on her cell phone. Actual *tears* pricked his eyes. Not the fake stuff he could call on at a moment's notice, but deep-seated pain in his heart with chest-constricting tears. He'd almost forgotten what they felt like.

Looking around the studio to keep her from seeing his

emotional drama, he noticed her camera sitting on the tripod, ready for the next photo shoot. If he had to leave her, he wanted to take his memories with him.

Kelly watched as he set up the camera. Her expression morphed from curiosity to shock. Her eyes widened and her mouth hung open.

She shook her head. "Are you out of your mind? Don't you know how sex scandals begin? Some horny idiot gets a bright idea, grabs a camera, and next thing you know it's all over the Internet."

"Not you. I trust you, Kelly."

"Famous last words."

"I want to remember this. I want to capture this moment so that no matter what happens in the next weeks or months or years, I'll always have you."

His words trickled out faster than he'd contemplated them. Now that he'd spoken the truth, he knew this was about much more than physical gratification. These last three weeks had changed him and he wanted something he could physically take with him when he left. Even thinking about the inevitable departure knocked the air out of his throat.

"I know you won't go with me, but your smile will. I can't take Pops back, but his wisdom will be with me forever. Every day here has been memorable. Please let me have proof this wasn't all a fabulous dream."

KELLY BLINKED AWAY tears and swallowed hard.

He crawled back in bed with the remote to the camera. It might have been selfish and reckless, but she was going to take whatever he wanted to give her. If all they had were great memories of the time they spent together, so be it.

"Forget it's there." Trevor leaned in and kissed her softly. The touch was so tender it broke her heart. Releasing the sheet she'd covered herself with, she ran her hands up his chest and around his neck. That body was so firm, so hot under her palms. "Focus on how good we are together."

Kelly bit her bottom lip and laughed. "Okay. On one condition."

"Anything."

"Can we position the pillows and blankets so that they cover everything?" Her bottom lip was going to bleed if she didn't quit biting it.

Trevor sighed dramatically. "This is what I get for falling for a photographer."

Kelly toppled him on the bed and kissed him silly. When she pulled back, he was still grinning. "Set the stage, woman. After that kiss I'm dying to love you again."

Kelly scrambled off the bed and looked though the camera lens at her bed. "The camera really does love you, Trevor."

"What about the beauty behind it?"

His question caused her hands to falter. There was no way to answer that question and keep her emotions in check. She went back to adjusting the camera. The picture would be great, but the lighting wasn't right. "We need candles."

"Hell, yeah, we do." Trevor bounced off the bed and Kelly couldn't help but appreciate the view of his naked body. Everything on him was toned and firm. One particular body part was incredibly firm indeed.

By the time the stage was set, Kelly was nervous. Her body hummed with desire, but the thought of capturing their love making on film was unnerving.

"You're thinking too much, baby." Trevor lay down on the bed and sprawled out.

"You're looking far too at home in my bed."

"It's a sexy bed." He held out his hand and enticed

her over. Kelly brought the camera remote to the bed and climbed on top of Trevor. With one final glance at the camera, she threw caution to the wind and settled over his hips.

As she and Trevor made love, the only sounds were the sighs of pleasure and the click of the camera. It was the craziest thing she'd ever done. No matter what else happened between them, she would remember this night for the rest of her life.

THE NEXT MORNING, Kelly was awakened by the sound of Trevor's voice. He was arguing with someone over the phone. She caught the gist of the conversation though. Whoever was on the other line was very unhappy with his leave of absence and wanted him back in California immediately.

"Fine," he growled into the phone. "Arrange a flight and text me the information. You'd better believe I'm not happy about this and someone is going to hear about it."

He turned around as she climbed out of bed and wrapped herself in a sheet.

"I'm sorry you had to hear that." He took a deep breath and put his hands on his hips. "I have to leave, Kelly. The studio and production company are threatening to offer the part to someone else if I hold up production because I haven't signed the contract. I've made a huge mistake by staying so long."

She didn't want to dissect that last sentence. Surely he wasn't referring to being with her. *Surely.*

Doing the only thing she could under the circumstances, she nodded and went to dress. "I'll fix you something to eat."

Trevor's forlorn sigh reflected exactly how she felt.

"Okay."

She couldn't show him how deeply she cared. There was an entire population of fans waiting for him to return and resume his place as Hollywood royalty. She'd known all along it wasn't smart to fall for him. The fact that she had was her problem, not his.

"One quick thing," she said as she raised her jeans over her hips. "Mark doesn't know we've been sleeping together. It's best if we keep it that way."

"Right."

Kelly threw on a sweatshirt and never looked back. She went to the kitchen and prepared Trevor's favorite food. If the magazines were right, he liked omelets for breakfast. Over and over again she repeated the reasons she couldn't be with him. He lived in Hollywood. She didn't. He lived in the spotlight. She didn't. Millions knew him. She was a nobody. He was cover model material. She wasn't.

"Whatever is going through your head is dangerous. I can practically see the hamster turning the wheel." Pops came over and kissed her on the forehead. "Your pretty boy leaving today?"

"How did you know?" Kelly focused on making the omelet.

"You think I don't remember being young, spending all day in your bedroom, not coming out for dinner? How do you think your father got here? I know exactly why you're beating the chicken out of those eggs."

If she weren't so upset, that would've been disturbing. She calmed her stirring motions.

"Pops." Kelly faced him and looked him dead in the eyes. "He has to leave. He's been here too long as it is. There is no other option. It's not like I can go with him." Her staccato sentences helped her control her emotions. "I will *not* lose my head over this. You have to promise that once he's gone, it's back to how it was. Life goes on."

Pops's white brows dipped down low and his lips pinched together. "Humph." He nodded. "If that's how you want it." He grabbed three plates from the cabinet. "You sure have been happy the last few weeks."

"Pops," she warned.

"Yeah, yeah, yeah." He scuttled to the dining room to set the table while muttering under his breath.

TREVOR WAS QUIET through breakfast. Kelly made his favorite. She knew him so well already. What he hated was the way she refused to look at him. It tore his heart out. Pops tried to make conversation and did a good job of diffusing the situation. They all ignored the big white elephant in the room.

After helping clear the table, he went to his room to pack his things. Jessica called with an afternoon flight itinerary. He was leaving from an airport over an hour away so no one would guess where he'd actually stayed. As he loaded his clothing, he realized that he'd have an entire hour in the car with Kelly to talk things over.

No matter what she was thinking, their relationship was *not* over. They had only scratched the surface, and if he had to have a damn press conference to announce it, she would get the point.

He thought about yesterday and it made his stomach do somersaults. Every touch, every kiss had branded his soul. There would be no other for him. He had to convince her if it was the last thing he did.

Downstairs, Kelly waited in the foyer with Pops. She wore a jacket, which was a good sign. Her keys still hung on the wall. Not a good sign. Pops came to him first, his hand held out.

"Son, I sure hate to see you go."

"I wish I could stay." Trevor shook his hand and pulled him in for a manly hug. "Duty calls. Thanks for…everything, Pops. You're one of a kind."

The hug had thrown off the old man, who nodded and looked away. "Come back when you can't stay so long, eh?" He chuckled and walked into the next room. The way his voice trembled nearly broke Trevor's will.

He turned to Kelly. "Ready to go?"

She inhaled deeply and opened the front door. Outside sat a cab. His heart sank down to his shoes.

"Kelly, baby."

"No." Her red-rimmed gaze found his and he longed to take her in his arms and make love to her once more. "It's easier this way. Please." She held out an envelope and asked him not to open it until he was alone.

"I'm going to call you when I get to the airport. Okay?"

"Yep." She stuck her hands in her pockets. This was the same woman who had met him at the airport three weeks ago, the woman who didn't know what to say or how to act around him.

"Kelly," he pleaded. "Don't shut me out. This isn't goodbye, do you hear me?"

She met his gaze. "We'll see."

"No, we won't." Trevor pulled her into his arms and brought her lips to his. He cupped her face and kissed her with all the passion and love he contained. That kiss left nothing unsaid.

When he pulled away, Kelly had tears running down her cheeks.

"This isn't over." He kissed the tears and touched his forehead to hers. "Don't give up on me, Kelly. I promise I'll be back as soon as I can."

"I hope you will," she whispered.

"I'll call you later. Don't cry, baby."

"Yep."

Trevor couldn't say anything. She waved at him once he was in the cab. He took out his phone and sent her a text. *I miss u already.* A reply never came.

All the way to California he racked his brain to come up with a solution to his problems. He had to deal with the studio and the movie. He had to convince Kelly he wouldn't forget about her.

Then he remembered the envelope in his bag. He slipped it open, looked inside, and made damn sure no one else could see. They were pictures from their weeks together. A sticky note clung to the first one with Kelly's elegant handwriting.

Trevor,

No matter what brought us to this point and no matter where we go from here, I will always cherish the time we spent together. I hope these pictures tell our story.

Trevor pulled out the pictures. The first one was of them in the woods on their nature walk. Kelly had argued when he suggested getting a picture of them together. Now there was her smiling face cheek to cheek with his. The next was him standing in her backyard with his knee propped up on the rock wall. Even now it dumbfounded him how she caught such amazing shots. The next one was with Pops and Mark sitting on the couch for movie night.

It struck him as sad that he didn't recall Kelly taking all these pictures. Now that he looked back, he remembered how she always had her camera with her. God, he missed so many chances to take her picture.

The last picture caused him to suck in a deep gulp of air. The shot was incredible. The candlelight danced off the gauzy white bedding that surrounded two lovers. They were forehead to forehead, wrapped in each other's arms. Kelly's perfect body was discretely covered with the duvet except for her shoulders. She straddled him and his arms held her tight, his hands pressing against her back. It was surreal. Looking at the amazing photo, he almost didn't recognize the couple as him and Kelly. They were perfect together. Both man and woman were smiling though their eyes were closed.

Love. That's what the picture said. This couple, caught in the moment of mutual ecstasy, conveyed deep resounding love for one another.

Trevor clenched his eyes shut; he refused to cry on this stupid plane. Since he'd seen the pictures of Ann and Gabe, gazing at each other in love, he'd envied the couple. Who would have thought he'd end up with something better? He pinched the bridge of his nose and took several deep breaths. Damn, but that woman had his heart in her hands. If she only knew what a mind-blowing experience the last weeks had been for him. His entire universe had shifted. The fulcrum of his thoughts had blonde hair and deep brown eyes and a laugh that resonated down to his bones.

He read her note once more. *I hope these pictures tell our story.*

Then it hit him. He knew what he had to do. With one text to his publicist, he set his plan into motion.

Chapter Eleven

FOR WEEKS, KELLY received texts and phone calls from Trevor on a daily basis. He kept his word and it meant more to her than she would ever admit. On their evening conversation a month later, he warned her that they were beginning to shoot and he might not be able to call every night, but he would text her as often as possible.

And so it ends.

Trevor was excited because he'd negotiated with the studio and got what he wanted out of it. Not that he gave her any details as to what "it" was. The filming schedule was grueling and kept him busy at all hours. The time zone difference didn't help. Eventually his texts declined. Kelly called him once or twice a week, but soon even that stopped.

Communication ceased and life as usual went on.

Six weeks after she'd said goodbye to Trevor, Kelly sat in a white paper robe in her doctor's office. She had a bandage in the crease of her elbow and her stomach was in a million knots.

"So you've been sick?" the doctor clarified.

Kelly nodded and described the symptoms; nausea, exhaustion, and migraines. She couldn't eat, couldn't sleep. Her body ached, and twice in the last week she'd had a light fever in the mornings.

"I think I caught some sort of stomach virus. Damn thing won't go away."

The nurse brought back the result of her blood tests, and Kelly watched with bated breath as the doctor read over the file. "Well, I know exactly what's going on, my dear. It's nothing to worry over."

"Good. So you can give me a prescription or something?"

"Kelly." He sighed and gave her a warm smile. "You're pregnant."

"Bullshit!" She clamped a hand over her mouth.

The doctor chuckled and showed her the results of her test. "Blood doesn't lie. You're pregnant."

Time stopped. The clock on the wall stood still as Kelly soaked in those words.

You're pregnant.

"Th—that's impossible. The surgeon told me I couldn't have children." She felt lightheaded and must have swayed because the doctor insisted she move off the bed and sit in a chair.

"At the time, you couldn't. Your surgeon was correct. However, that was right after your miscarriage. Haven't you been back for a checkup in the last two or three years?"

"No. I haven't had a reason. I haven't been with anyone since then."

The doctor's mouth twitched. "Clearly you've been with *someone*."

"I thought I couldn't." She started to sweat. "Oh, God." Kelly put her head between her legs, but it didn't do any good. A wave of nausea took her under until her world was spinning and black spots danced in her vision.

"Kelly, please take a deep breath. Oh, no."

Everything went black.

KELLY FELT LIKE a total fool as she walked out of the doctor's office. Not only had she fainted, but she'd stayed out for a long time. The doctor and nurses let her rest in one of the rooms until she could walk on her own and was capable of driving.

She didn't remember how, but somehow she managed to get home. Sitting in the driveway, she tried to figure out what to do. She was going to have a baby. After years of believing she couldn't conceive, years of thinking she would never hold a child born of her body, she carried life inside her.

A baby. Trevor's baby. A piece of him lived within her womb, the combination of their DNA. Would it have his eyes or his lips? Would it be tall like Trevor or short like her?

Her hand drifted to her belly. "I'll take care of you this time, baby. I won't let anyone hurt you."

Her phone rang and Mark's Bon Jovi ringtone was loud in the silence of the car.

"Mark?"

"Hey babe. Pops said you went to the doctor today. Been gone a while. What's up? You sick?"

"Mark." Her voice cracked as a new wave of tears fell down her cheeks. "I need to call in every favor I've ever done for you."

After a moment of stunned silence, Mark answered, "I'm on my way." Ten minutes later, he called as he entered her studio. "Where are you, babe?"

She rolled out of her bed and met him halfway into the room. Wrapping her arms around his neck, she let everything go. Mark held her tight as she wept in his arms. She cried so hard she couldn't answer his questions.

"Is it Pops? Kelly, is something wrong with him?" She shook her head. "Are you hurt? Did something happen? You've got to give me a clue. You're scaring me."

There was no way she could speak. Her tears kept coming until her head hurt and her eyes burned. Mark picked her up and sat down on the edge of her bed, cradling her like a child. He patted her hair and rocked her back and forth until she gained some sort of control over her crying.

"I've really screwed up this time."

"Kelly, babe, you've got to fill me in here. I have no idea what you're—"

"I'm pregnant." She started crying again when Mark went as still as the grave.

"You're p-p-pregnant? Who—" He cleared his throat. "Who's the father, Kelly?"

"You wouldn't believe me if I told you."

Mark put the puzzle together quickly. "It's Trevor Jacobs's baby, isn't it?"

Kelly nodded. She just couldn't look at him. Her face remained buried in his neck.

"Jesus. You never told me you two hooked up. I knew you two had chemistry, but you never let on it was more. I thought you couldn't have kids."

"At the time, I couldn't. But I never did any follow up appointments over the years because there was no reason to worry about it. I wasn't sleeping with anyone and I didn't date much."

"I guess you didn't bother with using protection with him, huh?"

"Obviously." Kelly climbed off Mark's lap and sat beside him on the edge of the bed.

"You have to tell him, Kelly," he said gently.

"I can't. Not right now. He's busy and he's working. I don't even know if he still cares about me, Mark. Honestly, I don't know how to mentally accept this pregnancy yet.

I've been looking into adoption agencies for years thinking I could never have a biological child. This baby is my personal miracle, but it might be his biggest mistake. Imagine what it would do to his career." Kelly began pacing the room. "Everyone would know. It would ruin him. He has this movie coming out and everything is going so well." She put her hands on her hips. "He might not believe me. He might think I'm a liar or some manipulative money grubber. He's been there before. I won't be the thing that ruins his life."

"And what about your life, damn it?" Mark stood and met her eyes. "Have you thought about what this will do to you? You're going to be a mother, Kelly. When people around town ask who the father is, what will you tell them? Have you thought about that? What about Pops? You think he won't put the pieces together?"

Kelly sat down in one of her winged back chairs and put her head in her hands. "I've already dealt with one scandal and lived through it. I can handle this too." She pushed her hair back and looked up at Mark as he walked around her living area. "I won't be the woman that ruined him, Mark. He deserves better. I would rather be a single mom than be the woman he can't get rid of because we have a baby together."

"How do you possibly know what he's going to do? This isn't a decision you can make for him. What if he wants the baby?"

"Exactly, Mark. What if he wants it? He can take it. With all his money and lawyers, he could rip this child right out of me. I can't lose another baby." She sobbed, wishing that memories of Craig and her miscarriage hadn't invaded her mind.

"I don't think he would be so cold, and neither do you. I meant what if he wants you and the baby? To have a family? You two obviously got cozy. Did he mention anything about seeing you again?"

"We kept in contact for a while, but he's been so busy. He's over it, Mark. Trust me. Anything he might have felt for me is gone. He'll hate me if this comes out." Kelly hid the fact she was the one that quit answering and returning his calls, not the other way around. It didn't matter; this baby didn't change anything between them. She absently rubbed her belly, wishing this child would be born into a real family.

Mark scrubbed his hands over his face and back through his long hair. He paced around her living area like a caged animal. Finally, he stopped and planted his feet. "Fine. If you won't tell people it's his," he said, swallowing hard, "you tell people it's mine. For now."

"What?" Kelly exclaimed. "Are you crazy?" The notion was preposterous. No one would believe the two of them would sleep together, much less have enough sex to conceive a child.

"You can't do this alone. God knows I'm not going to let you. Until you're ready to face Trevor, it's a cover story. We've been friends for years. It wouldn't surprise people one bit if we say we're having a baby."

Kelly leaned back in her chair and studied her best friend. Was he seriously going to do this for her? "Mark, you realize what this would mean for you?"

"It's not like too much would change, Kelly. Everyone in town thinks we're an old married couple anyway. When my friends invite me anywhere they all assume you're coming too. We've been together without being together for years."

"So you're going to pretend this baby is yours? What happens when word gets around? What about your over active social life—and by that I mean the steady stream of women and your man-whore tendencies?"

Mark began to defend himself, but Kelly zoned out. She covered her eyes with her hand and tried to mentally repel the oncoming migraine.

"Are you listening to me?" Mark demanded. "I mean it, Kelly, once you're ready, we call Trevor."

"Fine." She waved him off. "I have a headache. Apparently it's one of the side effects of this pregnancy."

That stopped his self-defense argument. "Are you okay? Can you take anything?" He knelt down in front of her and rubbed her knees.

"Tylenol. That's it."

"I'll get you some." Mark found the pills in her bathroom and poured her a glass of water. Once she swallowed them down, he propped up her feet and brought a blanket from her bed. "Why don't you get some sleep, babe? This problem doesn't have to be solved right this second. You don't look so well."

Kelly settled in her chair and pulled the blanket up to her chin. For a long time she and Mark sat in silence and watched the flames dance in the fire. How had her life come down to this? Her best friend was willing to ruin his life and tell people he knocked her up just so she didn't ruin the life of a worldwide celebrity—at least for a little while yet.

None of it seemed real. Inside her right now was the product of a whirlwind romance between a superstar and a recluse photographer. A baby grew where it shouldn't have been able. Her doctor warned her of the complications and possible bed rest. She was to call if anything at all worried her or seemed out of the ordinary.

Ha. Nothing about this situation was ordinary.

"I feel like all of this is my fault," Mark confessed. "If I wasn't such a douche and liar, Trevor would never have come here." He shook his head, his long hair falling to his chin. "I'm so sorry, Kelly."

"No one forced me to sleep with him, Mark. That was all my doing. Don't try to take the blame for my mistakes. Besides, I've always wanted a baby. And you have to admit, as far as fathers go, I did pretty dang good fishing in the gene pool." She laughed, pressed a hand to her belly. "This kid should be beautiful." The thought made her smile.

"Did he, I mean, how did this happen? I knew he was interested, but I never would have imagined you." He sighed, unable to find the right words. "Were you drunk?"

Kelly gave a sardonic laugh. "No, fortunately I was stone cold sober."

"Gross." He shook out his head. "Did you just want to bag a celebrity? Was that it? Or do you have feelings for him?"

Sadly, she couldn't get insulted at his insinuation. He wouldn't be the only person who jumped to that conclusion when this story got out. "I love him, as best as I'm capable of love these days."

"Does he feel the same?"

Kelly's eyes grew moist. "He asked me to go back with him. Said we weren't over just because he had to go take care of business."

"So he's in love with you?" Mark raised his eyebrows and crinkled his nose. His astonishment had her glaring.

"I know that's hard to believe—"

He blew out a deep gust of air. "That's not how I meant that. You're a very lovable person, Kelly. Give me some damn credit. I'm only trying to figure this out."

"Things started two days after he arrived."

Mark's jaw dropped. "So you two were going at it for three weeks?"

"Like rabbits." Kelly chuckled when Mark flinched. "Don't ask if you don't want to know. We made a baby, what does that tell you?" She sighed and gazed at the fire. "At first I thought he was acting, you know? I believed him by the end. Maybe that's my mistake. I don't know. But I'm not ready to tell him. I'm too scared of what he'll do."

"He's not Craig," Mark whispered gently, reading the

fear between her words. "He won't hurt you or the baby."

"My heart knows that." Kelly wiped at the tears on her face. "Once bitten, twice shy, huh? Just give me time. Right now all I can think about is keeping this baby safe, giving it the chance my other baby didn't get. Let me get a further along, please? No need to have everyone freaking out before I'm out of my first trimester. I could miscarry. This is a high risk pregnancy."

"You're my best friend, Kelly. Ever since Craig hurt you I've wanted to make it up to you somehow. Let me take care of you and the baby, at least until you're ready to call Trevor. When you're ready, we can do it together."

Fresh tears fell down her cheeks as she reached out for his hand. "You don't have to do this," she whispered with trembling lips.

"I love ya, babe. I'm not going to leave you alone on this ship. Besides, you owe me a kidney already. I might need a liver someday, too." Mark leaned in and kissed her cheek. "I'm going to run back to my place and pack some stuff. I'll be back."

"Mark, no."

"Shut up." He grinned at her. "Already so hormonal. This is going to be a damn carnival ride." He waved his hands in the air. "Whee!"

Kelly gave him the finger and they both smiled.

What had she ever done to deserve him? If there were any rhyme or reason in the world, she'd feel passion when she thought of Mark. Compared to the response she had when she thought of Trevor, Mark might as well have been her brother, not her former brother-in-law.

That was another mountain she would have to climb. After she sent their son to prison, Craig and Mark's parents weren't her biggest fans. They were upset about losing their grandchild, but not so much about losing her. How would they respond when they found out Mark was supposedly having a child with her? Something told her not to plan on being in any ugly sweater family Christmas photos anytime soon. Maybe they could keep his family in the dark for a few months.

The problems were snowballing. Everywhere she looked was another issue to tackle. Eventually they would have to tell Pops. He would know, damn his perceptive old ass. They wouldn't fool him. At least they wouldn't have to pretend. This house would keep her secrets.

Chapter Twelve

TREVOR ADJUSTED HIS sports coat and fixed a section of hair that had a mind of its own. The makeup artist dabbed powder on his face. He hated this part of television. He focused on the note cards in front of him. The statistics of battered women in the United States, the percentage of BDSM related injuries and divorces. He might not get the chance to talk about any of it, but he wanted to have these numbers ready.

"Mr. Jacobs? You're up after the next commercial break. Why don't you come on back?" The stage manager guided him back to the greenroom. He knew his way around the studio though. Every movie he'd ever been in was featured on this talk show. Larry, the host, was a friend. With a couple million viewers watching weekly, it was a prime opportunity to introduce fans to his new movie.

On impulse, he pulled out his cell phone and sent a text to Kelly. He hadn't heard from her in months. The last time he'd heard her voice was when she told him she would rather they not communicate any longer. She made it out to be for his benefit, but he knew something was up. Her tone didn't sound right.

Please watch the Larry Quinton talk show tonight. I'm

begging. I miss you so much.

After he sent the text, he prayed she obeyed him for once in their relationship. Damn, he needed her to watch. He needed her to understand.

The stage manager retrieved him and walked him to the edge of the curtain. He listened to Larry make a few jokes at his expense, all of which he laughed at. Then he walked confidently on the set and waved to the studio audience. The place was packed with women holding signs, wearing "I Love Trevor" shirts, and yelling at the top of their lungs. Trevor smiled, waved, and shook hands as he made his way to the interview chair. Even with all these women screaming for his attention, there was only one woman he wanted to give it to.

God, he hoped she was watching.

MARK PICKED UP her phone. His stomach dropped when he read the message. He figured the day was close when Trevor would find out everything and he dreaded the fallout.

Kelly was asleep when the text came through. She'd been sleeping a lot in the last months. It was like hibernation. The second trimester was over and her body was exhausted already. At seven and a half months, her condition was obvious and she wore those shirts that puffed out around the middle.

Even though he knew Kelly should tell Trevor everything, she still refused. She was so damned stubborn. The man was the real father of her child and she refused to acknowledge his existence.

He'd tried every Kelly-worthy trick in his playbook to make her pick up the phone. Nothing worked. Now Trevor reached out to her and he missed her.

Mark leaned over the bed they now shared and rubbed her shoulder gently. "Kelly, babe. Get up."

She grumbled and complained as she rolled over, her belly leading the way. "What?"

"We've been asked to watch a certain broadcast."

He grinned when she sat up and tried to smooth down her unruly hair. His best friend was crazy pretty even when she was cranky and hormonal and had a basketball under her skin. As much as he didn't want to get too cozy in his role as interim husband and father, every day he loved her a little more, cared a little deeper. At first it was easy to keep the distance between them. She was upset for weeks and he worked a lot.

Everything changed the first time they sat in the doctor's office and heard the baby's heartbeat. Kelly gripped his hand so tight it cut off circulation. It sounded like a horse galloping. The quick thu-thump of a heart beating inside her made everything real for him. And wasn't that a kick in the balls. It wasn't an abstract thought any longer. Kelly was going to be a mother. A baby grew in her and that baby would need a father.

A war raged within him ever since. It was unfair for Trevor to miss this experience, the heartbeat, the first sonogram, watching Kelly glow. He should have been the man sitting beside her getting the shit squeezed out his hand. Not Mark. Seriously, it had been painful. It should have been Trevor who brought her food when she was so sick she couldn't get out of bed in the mornings. God knows he couldn't cook. It should have been Trevor Jacobs who climbed in bed with her at night. As much as Mark had loved every minute of it, he was a substitute. Being second-string in the big game of life did a number on a man's ego.

Kelly loved Trevor. She was just too damned pig-headed to do anything about it. A couple days ago Mark had been working on her computer and found a file of pictures titled TJ. If a normal picture is worth a thousand words, these were worth ten thousand. The jealousy he felt had surprised him. As he scanned through the pictures of Trevor and Kelly making love, he grew angry with both of them, Kelly for pushing him away and Trevor for staying gone.

Maybe this interview would show them both the light. Was Trevor planning to come clean about their relationship on national television? Mark almost hoped so. It would piss Kelly off, but he was tired of living in the other man's place. It wasn't fair to him and it sure as hell wasn't fair to Trevor.

"I don't want to know." Kelly huffed like a spoiled child.

"Oh please. Don't even act like you haven't been stalking him online reading all the tabloids. Get your pissy ass up. We're watching this show." Mark hauled her out of bed and held her hand as they made their way into the den. Pops sat watching a western. "Hey, Pops. Can we change the channel?"

"Sure. I've seen this one a hundred times. Don't guess the ending is going to suddenly change now." He tossed Mark the remote.

Kelly curled up with one of the couch pillows. She and Pops had been distant since the night they sat him down and spilled their story about getting drunk and sleeping together resulting in her pregnancy. They never mentioned Trevor and never mentioned the fact she was too far along for their story to hold an ounce of truth. The old man had studied her, then Mark. His thick white brows dipped low as he exhaled slowly. He'd nodded, but said nothing else on the subject. All three of them had been living in a state of tension ever since. Pops knew, but no one said a word, especially not Kelly.

Mark flipped over to the right channel and the Larry Quinton Show jingle played. He flopped down next to Kelly and grabbed a beer from the cooler he and Pops shared. It was hard to stay mad at her when she scooted over and cuddled up under his arm. His hand instinctively went to rest on her belly. They could feel the baby moving now and it tripped him out.

Yeah, he loved her a hell of a lot. Too bad it wasn't enough.

"Tonight I have a man who has gone from Hollywood golden boy to Hollywood rebel," Larry announced. "He's no stranger to this stage. Please help me welcome back the one and only, Trevor Jacobs!"

Chapter Thirteen

KELLY DESPISED THE way her body heated as Trevor walked out for his interview. Dear God, he was every bit as handsome as she remembered. He looked so good with his fancy suit and charming smiles. The man knew how to dress the part as king of celebrities.

As he stood on the stage, waving at the loud audience, Larry Quinton laughed when the ladies kept chanting and applauding. "I should have had more security. You're going to cause a riot."

The two men shared a laugh and moved to sit down. Larry behind his desk and Trevor in a plush seat opposite him. "Wow," Trevor exclaimed, his face beaming with pride and amazement. Her heart clenched. That face was made for the spotlight.

"Thank you. Thank you so much. You guys are incredible." His response caused more applause and he shook his head, laughing.

"All right, all right, keep your panties on ladies, jeez," Larry said and chortled. The audience finally died down and Larry turned to his guest. "Is it like this everywhere you go these days?"

"Pretty much. I have enthusiastic fans." Trevor smiled

at the audience, who greeted him with more screams.

Kelly watched his carefree laughter, listening to the opening banter between him and the television host. Part of her withered inside. That was his life. That was who he was meant to be. Not the father of an unwanted child. "Do we have to watch this?" she asked Mark.

"Yep." He took a drink of beer and never looked at her.

She let out a huff and watched the screen again. This was going to be torture.

"So tell me about this project of yours that has everyone in Hollywood so worked up. You've caused quite a controversy."

"Yeah, well. That's Hollywood, all about the drama." Trevor let out a deep breath and began his story. "A few months ago, right after we finished the promotional tour for *Lethal Edge*—" He paused as the crowd cheered for his latest movie. "Thank you. It's a fantastic movie, great to do. Anyway, the studio hands me this script and says look it over, we think this could be your next big hit. I took it, ah, didn't really know what to think about it at first, and I knew that I needed a couple weeks to regroup, get my head in the right place."

"Your work schedule has been grueling lately," Larry agreed.

"Right."

"So you disappeared?"

"Best decision I've ever made."

"Where did you go?"

"A military bunker."

"Really?"

"No."

They laughed but Kelly let out a sigh of relief. "I will say it was...*exactly* the place I needed to be. I had the chance to look over the script, bounce it off someone who has a tendency to not hold punches."

"Someone outside the industry?"

"Yes. After that new perspective on the script, I," Trevor inhaled and exhaled, "I knew it wasn't anything I wanted to be associated with as it stood. I told them to make some changes or I was out."

"What changes?"

"What we ended up filming was nowhere close to what was presented to me. In my opinion, this film originally glorified the abuse of women under the guise of sexual exploration. Consensual or not, no woman should be treated like a rug to be trod on and beaten. I think when you strip it away to the bones of the film, that's what it was telling women. Put up with a man's abuse until he figures out how to love you properly. It's crap. Women deserve better."

The crowd came out of their seats with applause. Trevor tipped his head to them, but his smile was tight.

"How did the studio react to your demands?"

Trevor laughed. "It took some negotiating, like I said. Once I shared my vision with them, they were receptive."

"I bet." Larry looked down at his queue cards. "So after battling the studio, you decided to do something completely outrageous. Tell us about what happened next."

"I went on a mission to learn about the BDSM world, to figure out what it's all about and how it started and why it's so popular right now. Then I decided to show another side of the coin. The studio and I went back and forth daily for a couple weeks and in the end, we came up with something I'm quite proud of."

"You wrote, filmed, and edited in less than six months. That's almost unheard of in Hollywood." Larry was obviously impressed with what the actor had done.

Trevor nodded. "Oh, it was difficult. I had some amazing actors, writers, and production assistants that rallied to the cause. We wanted to make a buzz with this film."

"I'd say you've succeeded with flying colors. We have

a scene from the movie, why don't you set that up for us?"

"Yeah, this is a scene where the main character, Trish, is in the hospital after she experienced the negative side of this lifestyle and she's realized there is something deeply wrong with her husband, who is the aggressor in their relationship. My character, Blake, is her older brother, who is learning all this for the first time."

Kelly sat up and watched the screen with wide eyes. A woman sat on a hospital bed with two doctors in the room. The doctor examined her wrists where she'd been tied up. There were burns from the rope. Excuses flowed from the woman's mouth about how her sexual life was none of their concern. The scars on her back and neck were no big deal. They were some of the same excuses Kelly had given to her own doctors. Not that Trevor could have known that. Those were things she hadn't shared. Trevor's character was appalled, shocked by the revelation from his friend and comforting his little sister.

Kelly's heart raced and her breath quickened as she watched a scene from her own past being acted out on the screen. Only Mark's heavy hand on her shoulder kept her grounded.

"I'll be damned," Pops muttered from his recliner.

When the scene was over, the cameras showed Trevor and Larry again. "I had the chance to preview the movie, as did our audience. That's a powerful story. What was your inspiration?"

Kelly, Mark, and Pops had moved to the edge of their seats. Would he tell the world about her past? Was he capable of such treachery?

"Larry, I don't believe in coincidences. While I was looking at that first script, I did some research and found so many cases where women have been abused and even killed when the men in their lives turn something sensual into something sadistic. I want to be the voice for these women." A thoughtful smile crossed his face. "I want to be the kind of actor a woman would be proud of. Someone recently told me that I had more influence than I realized. It's time more actors used that power to bring awareness to our nation's issues. If it has to start with me, so be it. Anyone interested in getting involved to stop this kind of abuse can either go to my website or the movie's website to find more information."

The audience went nuts. They cheered and applauded. Kelly felt her bottom lip tremble. He'd heard her. He'd heard every word she said and he was making a difference.

"I have to ask," Larry began once the crowd was under control. "Because our female viewers want to know, is there a woman in your life?"

Trevor smiled brightly as the female audience members reacted to this question. "Not actively, no. But I'm waiting for that special woman to come around. Until then, I'm perfectly happy waiting until we both know it's the right time."

Kelly bit down the inside of her cheek to keep from crying. The taste of her own blood tinged her tongue. Larry finished up his interview and went to commercial break. She sat still, unable to move. Mark and Pops were silent beside her until her grandfather walked to the cabinet and pulled out a DVD.

"I guess we should watch this now. Jacobs sent it to me a couple days ago." He handed Kelly the case. It was Trevor's movie.

"Why didn't you tell me about this?" Kelly spit out with more volume than she intended.

"You're the one who set the tone here, Kelly Renee," he scolded. "You wanted to ignore his existence and I have. Don't get your knickers in a twist because I'm following your instructions."

Kelly went to argue, but shut her lips. He had a point. And he'd used her middle name, a sure sign he was in no mood to argue. They hadn't spoken about anything because she'd told him not to bring it up. This was all her doing. Truth be told, she was dying to see what Trevor had done.

"Fine. Let's watch it."

She put it in the player and sat back down on the couch next to Mark.

An hour and forty-three minutes later, the three of them were once again speechless. Kelly had tears streaming down her face. Mark was tensed and ready to combust. Pops had his mouth covered with his fist as he stared at the carpet.

"Son of a bitch." Mark wiped a hand down his face.

Kelly's stomach soured. Acid churned and rolled in her gut. She couldn't find the words to speak.

"The boy made a damn good movie," Pops said. Mark and Kelly whipped their heads around. "No one will ever know where he got the inspiration. Face it, he made a point with his film. And he played the noble role of hero."

"Are you serious?" Kelly screamed and popped to her feet. "He took my story, my history, my pain and humiliation and made a damned movie about it! The only thing he left out was the miscarriage. I can't believe *him*. And I can't believe you for sitting there and liking it."

"Kelly, he showed that bastard getting what he deserved. He brought attention to the fact that women can get hurt and no one should overlook it. It's a perfect example of how dangerous that bondage nonsense can become. Not even you can argue with that. You're letting your personal feelings get in the way."

Their conversation was cut off by Kelly's cell phone ringing. "Perfect. Just perfect." She pressed the answer button and spoke to her caller. "You bastard. How could you? Do you have any idea what a betrayal this is?"

"What? Did you even watch the movie? The interview? I'm trying to do what you told me to," Trevor argued over the line.

"No, you're trying to profit from my pain. I can't believe I trusted you."

"I'm not making a profit off your pain. Jesus, Kelly. Why are you acting so crazy about this? Didn't you read the letter that came with the movie? A portion of the proceeds are going to women's shelters and towards organizations promoting awareness of abuse."

Kelly stopped short. Too bad his motivations were trumped by the fact he'd taken her trust and thrown it away. "Good for you, Trevor. I hope that helps you sleep at night. But now every time I see your face, I'll remember that you took my personal life and plastered it on the screen for the world to gawk at." Her breath became labored and her head spun.

"Your story could help so many women, Kelly—"

"I can't do this." She hung up the phone and threw it at the wall. Pain streaked up her side and around her stomach. "Crap." She grabbed her side and Mark rushed over.

"Sit down, babe. This stress isn't good for the baby. You know you're high risk. You need to relax."

"I just pulled a muscle, Mark. I'm not dying." She fought off his hold.

"Hey. Don't take out your frustrations on me. I'm here, remember? Not him, *me*."

Kelly fell back on the sofa and pinched the bridge of her nose. It took a moment to let her cramp subside and she eased back into a sitting position. "I'm sorry. You're right."

"Why don't you go run a warm bath? You need to chill out." Mark helped her up and hugged her close. "I'm sorry, babe," he whispered in her ear.

"I should have expected as much."

"Kelly, come on." Mark sighed. He patted her hair and kissed her forehead. "I think he had good intentions."

"I have more important things to worry about. I'm going upstairs." Kelly tiptoed and kissed Mark, something they had begun doing for Pops's sake. He kissed her back, putting as much into it as he could. It really was a shame his body didn't stir with desire.

"I love you," he whispered before he let her go.

"I love you too." Kelly touched his cheek and turned away.

MARK CURSED AND sat back down on the couch. Pops watched him and he knew it. Pops finally huffed and groaned and grumbled until Mark asked what his problem was.

"Damn kids, must think I'm a basket full of stupid. You think I don't know that girl's in love with the movie star? Think I bought that bullshit about you two parenting that baby? You two couldn't create a romantic spark if you had a lighter, gasoline, and box of fireworks. That child is going to come out looking like that boy on the television and not a hint of you anywhere. How were you going to explain that one, genius?"

Mark chuckled. Of course the old man knew. He was nobody's fool. Even if they had been treating him like one.

"You know what really confounds me, son? I can't figure out if you're a sucker or a saint. How far are you going to go with this charade?"

"There's not too much I wouldn't do for her." Mark hung his head. "I'd stay with her forever if she needed me."

"I know you love her, son. But I have more passion for my morning coffee than what you two share. Guilt is a terrible foundation for a life together. You won't be doing that baby any favors either. How do you think it will feel when he or she finds out who its father is? It'll hate all of you. Use the brain God gave you, punk. After a few years you're going to grow bitter and wonder what your life could have been. What happens if you meet the girl of your dreams, Mark?"

"Believe it or not, Pops, before all this happened, Kelly was the girl of my dreams. We hung out, we went places together, she understood me, and I understood her. There was nothing and everything all in one. We had companionship without complications."

Pops laughed out loud. "If you want companionship without complications, get a damn dog. Not a wife and child."

Mark groaned. Pops was right. How did he fix this? He saw Kelly's phone lying on the floor. Miracle of miracles, it wasn't broken into a million pieces. "I guess I have a phone call to make, huh?"

"If you don't, I will." Pops stood up and held out his hand to Mark. "Do the right thing, son. Kelly will forgive you when she realizes it's for her own good and the good of that baby." He slowly made his way out of the den.

Mark stared at Kelly's phone for a long time. He prayed Pops was right about Kelly's forgiveness because if he made this call, she was going to be one angry, hormonal ball of rage. Recalling the last number on the phone he took a deep breath. Trevor answered on the first ring.

"Kelly? Oh God, baby, please don't be angry. Look, I'm getting on a plane. I have to see you."

"Trevor, it's Mark. Look, man, you and I need to talk."

Chapter Fourteen

KELLY SLEPT RESTLESSLY that night and it had nothing to do with her protruding belly getting in the way, though that didn't help. She tried sleeping on her right side, her back, and finally settled on the left side with four pillows strategically positioned. When she was finally comfortable, she looked over to see Mark staring at her.

"Did I wake you? I'm sorry." She reached out and took his hand. He brought it to his mouth.

"It's okay, babe. I didn't figure either of us would sleep tonight." He put his other arm over his eyes.

Kelly had noticed his restlessness in the last couple weeks. Each morning, he woke with the sun and went for an hour-long run through the hills. He would come back and take a shower before he had to leave for work. The airport had rearranged his schedule so he only had to work nights a couple times a week. Kelly reluctantly admitted she enjoyed those nights. Having Mark in her bed was both wrong and right at the same time.

They hadn't intentionally started going to sleep together, but after many nights crying herself to sleep, she'd asked Mark to hold her until she could rest. It was a matter of habit now. He still had his apartment and he hadn't technically moved in, but after six months, who cared about technicalities? In some states, they would be considered married under common law.

The one thing their relationship lacked was anything sexual. Mark had never instigated and neither had she. If she had to guess, that was the reason he wasn't sleeping. Her playboy had gone without sex for six months and was getting antsy.

"Mark?"

"Yeah, babe?"

"Do you, uh, would you feel better if you had sex?"

He turned his head and gaped at her like she had three heads. "Excuse me?"

"Never mind." She huffed and wished she'd never said anything. "It was a dumb suggestion."

"Kelly, I won't lie. After six months, I could use a good round between the sheets. Wait, you're not going to purchase me a prostitute are you? 'Cause I know you're not suggesting I sleep with you."

"Well, I guess I am. I know you're not used to going this long."

"If that's your version of seduction, I'm shocked as shit that you're pregnant." They both began to laugh and Kelly became tickled. The whole idea was ludicrous. Mark rolled closer to her and cuddled her. "Do you really mean with you? Can you even do that?"

"I'm pregnant, Mark. Not broken. We can…do other things…if you want. I mean, not that I'm really the best candidate to sleep with. But hell, I'm here."

"Oh, baby, you really know how to talk to a man," he deadpanned and nuzzled her neck as she giggled. "Be still my beating heart." He blew a raspberry against her skin.

"Oh my God. Stop being a dork. I'm just trying to help."

"Ah! I feel a stirring in my loins," he hollered with a

Scottish accent and tickled the spot under her ribcage that always made her giggle. She laughed harder until she had tears in the corner of her eyes.

"Watch it or I'll knee you in the loins."

His hands clapped over his crotch. "Please don't, lass, I happen to be very attached to my loins." They lay together until their laughter faded. Mark gazed down at her and pushed a strand of hair from her face. "I love to see you smile. You haven't done that much lately."

"Sorry. I've been hell to live with and you've been so amazing."

"It's nothing. I mean, your gassy-ness is gross, but— hey." Kelly punched his arm and he chuckled. "You need to remember something. Everything I do is for you and this baby."

Kelly leaned up on her elbow and smiled down at him. "I'll never forget what a great friend you've been. I really will give you a kidney."

"I'll need a liver first. You've driven me to drinking, woman." He chuckled and rubbed his chest. "Maybe I can have both. It'll be a matching set."

Her brows furrowed as she looked into his eyes. "Mark, I've never blamed you for anything that happened between Craig and me. You're nothing like him. I know that with every fiber of my being. Sometimes I have to wonder if you do, though."

The breath left his lungs and he blinked up at the ceiling. "Damn it, Kelly, now who's been watching too much Dr. Phil?"

She laughed and lay back down. "It's called mood swings. Give me five minutes and it will go away. I'll be back to my bitchy self."

Chapter Fifteen

THE NEXT MORNING Mark rose with the sun and left Kelly sleeping in the bed. The morning routine they had created worked in his favor today. Cell phone in hand, he took off to go on a morning run. While he was out, he called Trevor's personal number. Trevor was at a hotel by the major airport under the name Bauers. He'd rented a car so he could come to the estate. Both men knew Kelly was going to shit bricks when Trevor showed up on their front steps. He'd be pissed that Mark hadn't mentioned the whole pregnancy thing.

Sometimes the less people knew, the better…at least for now. The moment Trevor laid eyes on Kelly, he would get the picture.

Kelly was getting out of the shower when Mark came back. "Morning, babe!" He kissed her forehead and cupped her cheek. "How are you feeling today?"

"I'm okay. Feeling a bit awkward after last night." She stepped away from him, comfortable even though only a towel was draped across her chest. "Did I cross a line? I don't want things to be weird because I made this arrangement something you don't want it to be. Mark, you can go out and do your thing. It's not like we're married—"

"Kelly." He shut her up with a chaste kiss. "I'm cool. We're cool." *Not that it's going to matter in the next couple hours anyway.* "Look, why don't we have breakfast with Pops out on the patio? You can bring your camera, take some of those flowery, estrogen-filled pictures you like."

She nodded and her expression warmed again. "I thought I should take some pictures of myself, you know, with the baby bump." She lovingly ran a hand over her belly.

Mark reached out and followed her hand. Even if it wasn't his child that grew in there, the little guy or girl was special to him. "I think that would be great."

"I'll go fix breakfast." Her smile was genuine and that was the prettiest thing he'd seen lately.

A few minutes later, he sat on the patio with Pops while Kelly dished out food. The way she carried on about a recent photo shoot was clearly her way of avoiding the subject of last night. Pops listened, but kept eying Mark and his watch all through breakfast. He hoped Kelly didn't notice how tense they both were.

When Trevor still didn't show up, Mark suggested Kelly go into the sitting room and read while her food digested. Heartburn was a real problem at this stage and she needed to take it easy after such a large meal. It would also put her closest to the front door.

He volunteered to clean up the breakfast dishes. Mark had his hands in the soapy water when he heard the doorbell. It took monumental control to stay in the kitchen. But when he heard a feminine scream and the front door slam, he took off running.

Kelly stood in the entry, her hands over her mouth, staring at the closed door.

"What is it?" Mark asked, taking her shoulders in his hands.

"Kelly," called Trevor from outside. "Open the door, baby. You can let me in or I'll bust in."

"What in the devil is going on down here?" Pops made his way down the stairs.

Kelly shook her head wildly and backed away from Mark. "No. He can't be here. He's going to be so mad at me."

"Kelly." Mark sighed. "It's time." He opened the door and Trevor rushed in. Without so much as a hello to anyone else, he took Kelly in his arms and kissed her.

Mark watched as his best friend slowly returned the kiss, slowly raised her hands to his collar, and eventually pulled him closer.

He turned away. The heartbreak of the moment was unexpected.

"Now that's how you spark a fire," Pops muttered from beside him, his white eyebrows high on his head.

Mark couldn't compete with that. On some level he didn't understand, it shattered him. In the recesses of his brain, he'd actually begun to get comfortable in Trevor's shoes. Now that bubble was burst. Even knowing Kelly wasn't meant to be his, he'd grown closer, more invested. That was a foolish mistake on his part. The truth of it punched him in the gut.

TREVOR KISSED KELLY with all the passion and zeal he'd built up over the last few months of not seeing her. He didn't think or pay attention to who might have been in the house to see them. His quick movement caught her off guard, just like he wanted. Damn, how he'd missed her. Not communicating had been agony. Hearing her anger on the phone last night had torn his heart out of his chest. Nothing could have kept him away, even before Mark told him to come.

He slipped his arm around her lower back and pulled her closer. She resisted at first, but eventually leaned into him. That was when he noticed something was different. Her stomach pushed against his *a lot*.

Kelly broke their kiss when he tried to reach down and touch the bulge he hadn't noticed in his rush to kiss her. "Stop." She backed away. The way she stared with such painful longing was killing him.

His eyes followed the movement of her hands. Kelly covered her belly protectively. He saw what he'd missed in his moment of crazed kissing.

"You're—" He looked at Mark, Pops, and back to Mark. "Yours?" He took a step towards the other man, hell bent on pulverizing his head if the answer was yes.

Puffing out his chest, Mark looked him dead in the eyes. "Nope. *Yours*."

His. Kelly was pregnant with *his* child. Trevor ran his hands over his head. Could this be possible? They'd been together numerous times, but she'd said a pregnancy couldn't happen. He'd been foolish enough to believe her. "You lied?"

Kelly threw her hands up in the air and glared at Mark. "See? This is why I didn't want to tell him yet." Then she turned her angry gaze to him. "Of course that's your first thought. No, I didn't lie." Kelly seemed to gather herself. "I didn't think it was possible. I was wrong. Obviously." She pointed both hands at her belly and crossed her arms over it protectively. "Trust me, the next time they suggest follow up consultations, I won't ignore it."

"Why didn't you tell me? My God, Kelly. We've talked since this happened. You never said a damned word. How could you keep this from me?" Trevor thought he might faint. Talk about a kick to the balls. He was going to be a father. He reached out and braced himself against the wall, bent at the waist. "Oh, shit. Is the room spinning for anyone else? Seriously, I think I might be sick."

"Welcome to my world," Kelly scoffed.

"Come on, son." Pops slapped him on the shoulder and guided him into the sitting room. A surge of jealousy spiked through him when Kelly sat next to Mark on the opposite side of the room. That was his woman, the mother of his unborn child, and she couldn't even sit by him.

He repeated his previous question to Mark this time. "I think a head's up would have been nice."

"I didn't want you to freak out and bail." Mark flinched when Kelly turned her glare in his direction.

"I meant months ago, damn it," Trevor growled at Mark.

She gasped and popped to her feet. "You talked to him?"

"This is for the best, Kelly." He instinctively put his hands over his crotch.

She looked at Pops, whose lips thinned into a scowl. "You too?"

Her grandfather tugged Mark off the couch. "Let's leave them to it. 'Cause she *will* shoot the messenger."

"No, Mark. I thought we talked about this. We agreed that I would decide when to tell him."

"It's past time. You know that." Mark held her by the shoulders and touched her cheek. Their easy affection burned in Trevor's gut. "We got too comfortable, Kelly. You and me playing house isn't going to work anymore. I'm tired of being his stunt double. You need the real father of this child, not me."

"I'm sorry, you *what*?" Trevor stepped up to Mark. Images of barefoot and pregnant Kelly kissing Mark as he came home from work sent his temper through the roof. Every muscle in his body tensed. "What the hell does that mean? Playing house?"

Mark rolled his eyes. "Back off man, I'm just taking

care of my friend."

"Yeah, he was here. Unlike you," Kelly said.

"So that's how it is? You thought you would step right on up and take my place?" Trevor might not have been around the last few months, but Kelly was his and that baby in her belly damn sure was. Mark had no right to keep him from it.

"It's not like that." Mark met his challenge and nudged Kelly behind him. "Kelly needed someone."

"And here comes her hero. Ready to save the day once again. Is that why she didn't call me? Because you just have to be the savior every time she gets in a bind. Is this your fault? This entire house is full of liars."

Mark reared back and threw a punch right to Trevor's jaw. Kelly screamed as Trevor recovered. That was all it took to push him over the edge. This sonofabitch kept Kelly and their child hidden. He wasn't about to let Mark ruin his chance at a family. As soon as he found an opening, he knocked Mark in the gut, folding him over in pain.

Mark might have been taller and wider, but he didn't have the years of martial arts training that Trevor did. Mark would swing and miss; Trevor would duck and hit. It wasn't enough to seriously hurt him, but it did slow him down. If he put Mark in the hospital, Kelly would hate him for sure. But that didn't stop him from beating his nose in.

He had Mark on the floor and was ready to knock the asshole out cold and end this shit. He reared back and his elbow caught something but he didn't care. The blow he delivered knocked the fight out of Mark. His opponent went slack, groaning as he rolled over to his side.

Trevor got to his feet and wiped the blood from his knuckles. His ears rang and his heart pounded out of his chest. This was nothing like practicing with his personal trainer. That was child's play compared to a real fight. Adrenaline flowed through him right along with his anger.

He barely heard the sniffles behind him over his labored breathing.

When he turned, he saw Kelly on the floor, holding her hands over her face. Her fingers were bloody. Pops knelt next to her to help her sit up.

It took Trevor a second to realize what had happened. That's what his elbow had banged into. *Shit.* "Oh hell! Kelly." He reached for her, but she crawled away, hiding behind Pops.

She held up one hand to ward him off and the other protected her stomach. "Don't hurt me. I'm sorry, please don't hurt the baby. Please." She covered her face and her stomach with her arms, bracing for an impact that would never come. Over and over again she sobbed and pleaded for mercy. "Don't hurt the baby. I'm sorry I got pregnant. Please, don't kill the baby."

The entire scene halted. Her words struck the men in the room like a wrecking ball. Kelly wasn't in the same place with them. Not mentally. She was stuck in her past, reliving the nightmare from years before, doing everything she could to protect the innocent baby in her belly.

All three men reached for her. Trevor was the closest but she scrambled away and called out for Pops, begging him not to beat her. Even Mark was met with sobs and pleading.

Trevor blanched and froze where he knelt. His brows drew up and his mouth hung open. She thought he was going to hit her? Her fear knocked the breath from his lungs. Kelly cowered behind her grandfather like a child. Dear God. He would never hurt her on purpose. Didn't she know that?

"Son," Pops said softly. "Why don't you just leave? I think she's had enough for one morning."

"Yeah." Mark spat from behind him. "You're good at leaving. Should be simple to do it again."

"You too, punk."

"Me? What did I do?"

"You threw the first punch." Pop's voice held authority the younger men recognized. "Now both of you clear out of here before you upset my granddaughter more than you already have."

Mark stomped off and the sound of the back door slamming made everyone flinch.

"Kelly," Trevor whispered. He wanted to beg and plead but he was so damned angry at everything. How had their reunion turned to shit so fast? "I'm sorry, baby. Can you hear me?"

It took her a moment to figure out where she was. Her wide eyes darted around the room and her hands pawed at Pops when she recognized his face.

"I'm here sweetheart, you're okay." The old man shushed her until she nodded and was able to stand up. She rubbed her hands over her stomach over and over again, nodding as if to reassure herself that she was still carrying the child.

"Kelly? Baby?" Trevor's voice cracked, but he didn't care. Seeing Kelly so out of her element of mental control shook him to his core. She'd suffered more at her ex-husband's hands than she'd let on. He might never fully understand what she'd been through.

"Just go," Kelly said. Her face crumpled and she turned into Pop's shoulder. "I can't do this. I can't see him."

Trevor ran both hands through his hair and clenched his eyes shut. What else was he supposed to do? Staying against her wishes would only cause her more grief. She clearly didn't want or need him here. "If that's what you want, baby. I'll go."

Trevor drove his rental car around town for hours. That couldn't have gone worse if he'd scripted it. All he wanted was to prove to Kelly that he loved her and that he hadn't broken her trust. But he wasn't the one withholding vital information. A baby. *God*, How else was he supposed to react? He was going to be a father. If Kelly would even let him. This changed everything. The hub of his universe had shifted.

What would he do now? Kelly might not want him, but he couldn't walk out on his kid. Should he call his lawyer about getting joint custody? If Kelly fought him, he would fight back.

He cringed thinking about her busted lip, how fragile and small she'd looked huddled up behind Pops, cradling her swollen belly.

Don't kill the baby.

Trevor slapped the steering wheel. He might have hit her on accident, but it didn't matter. She's mentally classified him with her ex. It had been written on her face, she couldn't even look at him.

Months of pain and secrets lay between them, creating a great chasm in their relationship. He didn't know if it was possible to patch it up. Kelly had kicked him out of her house. She'd kept a massive secret for months, she'd ignored his calls, and she'd been shacking up with Mark in the meantime. Maybe it was over after all.

He picked up his cell phone and made a call as the first drops of rain hit his windshield. Parked in the grocery store lot, he called the only person he knew to call.

"Dad?"

"Trevor? Hey son. I was just thinking about you. Hold on, let me go into the next room so she won't hear."

It burned him that his father had to hide from his step-monster. But that was nothing new.

"I need some advice." Trevor gave his father the rundown of what happened. It was a long and exhausting conversation with his father asking questions about lawyers and scandals.

"Run, Trevor. I'm telling you, son, you don't know that

this girl is telling the truth. You said yourself that other guy was there with her."

His heart crumpled at the thought of never seeing Kelly again, of never knowing their child. Was his father right? Could he really believe her? He remembered back to the afternoon they sat in her bed and she showed him the African child advocate agency she'd been donating to. They talked about what it would take to adopt a child. That woman, the woman he'd fallen in love with wasn't capable of scandalizing him. He believed in her.

"I trust her, Dad."

"Haven't you learned anything from your line of work? Don't trust anyone. This woman pops up pregnant when she told you she couldn't. I can smell the ink of the tabloids now."

"She didn't contact me though. I came to her. If I hadn't come back, I don't know if she ever would have told me."

"Then you're the fool for not staying away." He talked in a hushed voice. "Son, I'll admit, the thought of you settling down and popping out a couple grandkids for your old man is a nice thought." He stopped to yell at his wife in the other room. "You are not too young to be a grandmother. Just because your tits are only ten years old doesn't mean the rest of you is. Mind your own goddamned business." He groaned and Trevor could hear the utter exhaustion in his father's voice. "As I was saying. That life sounds nice. But you didn't sign up for that. You signed up for a life of publicity not privacy, of constant public scrutiny. You really think that little mountain maid is going to adjust? You think she'd going to stick around once she's had her fifteen minutes of fame and stuck you with outrageous child support? Listen to me when I tell you that women are calculating and manipulative. She's going to be a pain in your ass."

"I can't walk away. I love her, Dad."

"Love?" his father said and laughed. "Love is a joke,

Trevor."

"Are you saying you never loved Mom?"

There was a beat of silence then a sigh on the other end of the line. "Your mom was one of a kind, Trevor. She loved me when I was poor and worthless. Why she stooped to marry me, I'll never know. But that didn't last and look what the hell I'm stuck with now. Men like us, rich men, don't find love. You're around beautiful women all the time. Don't settle down with just one. And don't get stuck with the kid if you don't know for a fact it's yours. It will ruin your career. You get your ass out of there and tell her if she wants anything from you, the request better come with a DNA test."

Maybe his father was right. If this surfaced, it would ruin all their lives. Kelly and Pops would forego privacy, he would end up with some outrageous child support and the tabloids would have a field day. As much as it hurt to think about never being with Kelly again, he couldn't do anything else to bring her pain. He would send money for their baby, and leave her alone just like she asked.

Trevor pointed the car towards the airport and let the tears fall. He loved Kelly enough to do what was best for her, even if it meant living in pain for the rest of his life.

Chapter Sixteen

POPS HELPED KELLY up and they held each other as Trevor once again walked out, slamming the door in his wake. Her past was too close to the present and if she saw Craig in Trevor's face, she might not ever be able to separate the two. Unable to take much more, she broke down and sobbed on her grandfather's shoulder. He led her to the kitchen and wet a cloth for her face.

"I've really screwed up this time, huh?" She wiped her eyes and then her bloody lip. It was a minor injury, but it stung. Trevor had knocked her off her balance more than he'd actually hurt her. Her heart knew that, but her head went back to the last time she'd been knocked to the floor by a man. How many times had she been in that same situation, huddled up in the fetal position on the ground? Even though time had healed the scars, she could still hear Craig screaming and feel his shoe as it rammed into her stomach.

She'd been so lost in the past, she'd been absorbed in the pain, sucked back to that day. How could she have thought Trevor would hurt her like Craig did? He wouldn't hurt a soul. But her instincts had taken over. All she cared about was protecting her child from another threat. She couldn't risk losing another baby. She'd never recover if it happened again.

Trevor wasn't Craig, nowhere close. She had to get her head in the right place. Trevor was stricken when he'd hurt her, an emotion her ex-husband never felt.

Pops inhaled deep and let it out with a shaky sigh. "I'm not going to blow smoke up your dress, sweetheart. You've made some bad choices and now you have to clean up the mess." He went to the fridge to get ice.

"I don't know how to fix it. I thought I was doing the best thing for everyone. Now? Now I don't know what to do. I totally lost my shit in front of Trevor. He probably thinks I'm a lunatic. When Mark reached for me, all I saw was Craig's face. They're brothers, how could I not? Mark already deals with guilt over Craig. He must hate me right now. I've hurt everyone I love, Pops."

So many times she imagined Trevor coming back, taking her into his arms and loving her. None of those times included a fistfight with Mark or a flashback to when she'd been beaten. How had things gotten so out of hand?

"Are you saying you love Trevor?" Pops looked into her eyes and held a cold compress on her lip.

For the last few months she and Mark had done a piss-poor job of acting like Trevor was out of the picture. Her grandfather was no fool, though. Knowing that he knew the truth didn't make it easy to confess. She nodded her head, fresh tears formed in her eyes.

"What if he doesn't love me back? What if he's too angry about the baby, Mark, all of it?"

"It seems to me, you're asking the wrong man the questions."

Kelly hung her head and rubbed her belly. "What if he's gone for good this time?"

"Then I guess you'll have your answers." Pops kissed her forehead. "And the punk won't stay mad forever. It's not his style."

Late that afternoon, she sat in the bay window and watched the rain streak down the glass. Her biggest fear had come true. Trevor found out about their baby and walked away. It had been hours and no sign of him. Unlike Mark, who had simply stepped outside, Trevor *left*. Mark called and the hotel confirmed Mr. Bauers had checked out. He was most likely on a plane back to his normal life.

She closed her eyes and rubbed her aching temple. Her child would grow up always seeing its father, but never knowing him. That's what she mourned now. Until today, she'd had hope that Trevor would be an active father to their baby. In the back of her mind, she'd been certain Trevor would love her enough to forgive her and come back into their lives. All her hope was gone now.

A car drove past on the road. For a second, her heart stopped but the car didn't break or slow down at her driveway's entrance. A ping of disappointment struck. She had to accept that Trevor was gone.

She rubbed the kicking bulge in her belly and prayed her child would one day forgive her for robbing him or her of a father. "I'm sorry, baby," she whispered through her tears. "It's all my fault." Once again, she hadn't protected her child. This time it would be her baby that paid the price. That hurt her more than the thought of being alone.

Kelly had never known her parents and their loss was hard enough. Her child would know that he or she had a dad, but he'd rejected the chance to be there for them. The daunting reality of being a single mother weighed on her whole body, making her ache down to the bone. She rubbed at her sternum and hugged her belly. No matter how hollow she felt inside, she would have to be everything to her child: mother and father, friend and foe, teacher and disciplinarian.

Another set of headlights shined down the road, glinting off the glass of the windows. This time they turned and came barreling up the driveway. Her breath caught and she reached up to the window to touch the glass. *Please God, please be him.*

Trevor slid out of the car into the pouring rain. He took two steps before he looked up and saw her sitting in the window.

He'd come back.

"Well, well, well," Pops said from the entry hall. He smiled at Kelly. "Looks like you have your answer."

She bolted to the front door, as fast as a heavily pregnant woman could anyway. When she opened it, Trevor stood in the same spot on the walkway getting drowned by the rain. Kelly went to the edge of the covered patio and hugged herself.

"What are you doing here?" she called over the sound of rain and thunder. "The hotel said you checked out."

Trevor was drenched. His clothes stuck to his body, his hair dripped in his face. But he made no move to come out of the downpour. "I was halfway to the airport when I turned around. I couldn't leave you. Not again. I love you, Kelly."

How she managed more tears, she'll never know. But this time, they were tears of happiness and overwhelming relief. "I love you too. Please come out of the rain."

Trevor shook his head and opened his arms to the sky. "I'm letting it wash everything away. I want to start clean, to start over with you and our baby. Can we do that? Please?" His voice cracked. It was hard to tell in the rain and the darkness, but Trevor was crying. His lips trembled and his eyes were bloodshot.

He loved her. He wanted her. He wanted their baby. That was all she'd prayed for. No matter where they went from here, at least she knew that Trevor loved her. He'd come back.

"Are you sure you're up for this role? Fatherhood isn't exactly scripted. God knows we have a lot to work out."

"I promise you, it will be my best performance yet, the

role of a lifetime. I'll give it everything I have."

Kelly stepped off the porch and into the spring rain. When she reached Trevor, she held out her hand. "I'm Kelly."

"I'm Trevor." He smiled and slid his hand into hers.

"I'm pregnant."

"Man, you move fast for a chick I just met."

Kelly put her hand over her mouth, but she couldn't hold in her laughter. Even though she was crying, they were tears of joy and hope.

Trevor pulled her into his arms, one hand on her back, the other on their child. "I'll do anything you want, just please let me be this baby's father and your husband."

Kelly's face dropped. *"That's* your proposal?" She slapped his chest. "I'm standing in the rain looking like a drowned cat and you pick *now* to propose?"

Trevor looked to the heavens and groaned. "You're going to drive me crazy, aren't you? Can't you answer the question?" He leaned his forehead to hers and held her face in his palms. "Forget what the picture looks like and just say yes."

Kelly's heart flipped in her chest. Seeing his smile again turned her inside out. All this time she'd waited, fearing what he would do. Not once did she imagine he would want to marry her. Could they make it work? They were going to have a baby, she was damned sure going to try.

She linked her arms around his neck. "Yes."

Trevor closed the distance between their lips, kissing her so thoroughly even the rain couldn't cool her off.

"You know," Pops hollered from the porch. Mark stood behind him with towels. "You can do that inside—where it's dry."

Kelly and Trevor laughed and made a mad dash for the foyer.

"Welcome back." Mark passed Trevor a towel.

"You could have said that earlier, instead of that right hook." Trevor grinned back.

Mark rubbed his bruised jaw. "If I would've known you were a freaking ninja, I might have."

Trevor held out his hand and Mark shook it. Something passed between them and their fight was over. Thank God, otherwise Trevor would hit him again when he found out Mark was the baby's godfather. They should probably have that conversation soon.

They spent the rest of the evening with Pops and Mark catching up on the last six months. The tension between the leading men in her life was thick, especially Mark and Trevor. The level of devotion Mark had shown her over the months was not unnoticed. Each time they shared a private detail about her pregnancy or her moods, she could see Trevor's jaw clench. He was trying so hard not to be jealous, but there was so much Mark had experienced instead of him.

On the opposite end of the scale, every time she smiled at Trevor or touched him, Mark would turn his head away or ask Trevor an off-the-wall question to veer them off track. Kelly was a tree between two dogs. She blamed herself. Both men meant the world to her and both men wanted to be number one. The fistfight might be over, but they were a long way from being besties.

"Well, I'm going to head out." Mark stood up and brushed down his pants. "I have the late shift tonight so don't wait up." He rubbed a hand over his face and scratched at his chin. "Um, I guess I can move back to my apartment now." His shoulders slumped a fraction.

"I'll walk you out." Kelly reached for his hand and allowed him to pull her up. They went to her studio, the room they had shared for months. "I can't imagine how weird this is for you."

"I'm the one who called him, Kelly. It's way past time for him to be here. I guess I didn't think much further ahead, though." He shrugged it off.

"Mark…"

"Don't. Please. For the love of my dignity, don't give me some apology and words of consolation. I've already had my ass handed to me. My balls are about to shrivel up like raisins. Let's call it what it is. You're my best friend, you'll always be my best friend, and nothing will change that. Now we can get back to normal."

"Yep."

"Oh no, not the one word sentences." His laughter held bitterness in it. "I don't belong in this picture, Kelly. You're the photographer. You know that. *One of these things is not like the other*," he sang playfully. They both grinned, even though her chest ached for him.

"I love you."

"Oh, babe." Mark pulled her in for a hug. "I love you too." He gave his best grin, but it didn't meet his eyes. "Now you can be happy in a relationship that was meant to be. And I can go get laid."

Kelly's startled laughter broke the serious mood. "You really are a man-whore at heart."

"After six months of celibacy, I plan to be."

"I'm *not* baby-sitting." Kelly stuck her finger in his face. They hugged once more until she could bear to let go.

Mark reached down and picked up his duffle bag. He held it up. "What does this tell us?"

She'd never even thought about the fact he kept his clothes in a gym bag and not in her dresser or closet. Why hadn't she noticed that sooner? After six months, he'd never actually moved in. Even his toiletries were in a travel bag on her sink. *Wow.* That revelation blew her mind.

"I guess you're right. We were only playing house." That was a shame. Mark would make a wonderful husband if he treated his wife half as well as he treated her.

"I'd do it again in heartbeat." He studied her for a moment. "We're good, Kelly. I'm not upset and you shouldn't be either. Trevor's a good man with good intentions, even if his execution needs guidance."

Kelly's throat closed up and she didn't trust her voice, so she simply bobbed her head and looked at the floor. She couldn't see her shoes anymore and that upset her too.

As Mark's truck pulled out of her driveway, she heard the laughter coming from Pops and Trevor inside the house. Her life had once again done a ninety-degree turn, veering off the course it was on but not going back to what it was before Trevor stepped off that plane. Only time would allow things to get back to normal with her best friend.

That night, Trevor walked Kelly to her studio and shut the door behind them. It was amazing how nervous she was to have him in her space again. Circumstances were so different now. There was so much left unsaid between them.

"That's still the sexiest bed I've ever seen." Trevor touched her duvet and smiled up at her. Dear Lord in Heaven, he could melt diamonds with that smile.

"It's been a real godsend in the last couple months. My back has been killing me." She reached around to rub her spine and her belly protruded out further.

"I can't stop staring at you. It's so hard to believe you're pregnant with our baby even though I can see it, feel it."

"You want to hear it?"

His face lit up. "Can I?"

Kelly retrieved a home fetal heart monitor. She sat down on the bed and wiggled herself into place, lifting her shirt to reveal the bump. Her eyes went to Trevor's face, fearing his reaction to her bloated state. "I look a little different than last time you saw me."

"So?"

"It doesn't freak you out? I'm not the prettiest prego woman. I look like I ate a basketball."

Air left his mouth in a gust. "Are you kidding me? I'm

so damn nervous and excited, I can't stand it. Show me how this thing works."

Kelly relaxed slightly and turned on the Doppler. She rubbed the blue gel on her belly and pressed the probe to her skin. She could guess about where the best spot. It took a few minutes, but finally they heard the quick thump-thumps of their baby.

"Oh my God." Trevor had both hands on her stomach, his eyes were huge and filling with moisture. "Holy shit. That's our baby. We created a life." He laughed, the tears spilling down his cheeks. "That's my kid in there."

His happiness and joy were all she'd ever wanted. This moment was what she'd dreamed of for months. Trevor was falling in love with their little one.

They heard a thump that was out of place.

"What was that?" Trevor asked with child-like enthusiasm.

"He kicked the probe because I was pushing on it."

Trevor's laughter was medicine, like addictive balm to her damaged heart. He kissed her belly. "Already as pushy as his mother. You think it's a boy?"

"I'm carrying low. Some say it means a boy. Not always." She shrugged. "I'm surrounded by pain in the ass men, so why wouldn't it be another one?"

"What's it like to be pregnant?"

"Why? You thinking about giving it a go?" Kelly giggled as Trevor rolled his eyes. "It's cool. I can feel the baby. My skin is fabulous, my hair is growing like crazy, and my boobs are freaking massive." Trevor noticed and wiggled his eyebrows. "I have to warn you though. I'm practically combustible. I have heartburn every night and I can burp like a full-grown man. Not to mention that I piss like a Russian racehorse every five minutes. Hell, I have to pee right now."

Trevor threw his head back and laughed. "I'll deal."

He pushed himself up so he could kiss her. In the blink of an eye, she was up in flames. What started out as a mild make out session quickly turned into fevered rubbing and caressing.

"Trevor," she whispered against his lips. "I need you to know something." She put a steadying hand on his chest. "I'm sorry. I should have called you the moment I found out about the baby. I was so confused and excited and terrified. My biggest fear was that you would think I had purposefully deceived you and that you would be angry and…" She looked away. It seemed too stupid now to think that Trevor would ever hurt her, but at the time, that's how she felt.

Trevor gathered her close and kissed her head. "We've both screwed up. I shouldn't have stayed away. I gave you every reason to doubt me. But I'm here now, and I'm not leaving again."

Kelly touched his cheek, reveling in the way he gazed at her with pure adoration. "You're going to have to take care of things in California, Trevor. I know that. Just promise that you'll always come home to me."

"I promise. I love you." Trevor kissed her until her toes curled. How she'd missed his lips, his touch.

Kelly tugged his shirt over his head and ran her hands over his muscular chest. "I've missed you so much. Nothing was right without you." Her body hadn't been so alive since the last time he'd caressed it. Trevor's hands stroked and petted her until she thought she would burst into flames. Being pregnant made everything sensitive. She could get used to that.

"Can I make love to you?" Trevor panted against her lips.

"Not exactly, but I'm willing to get creative." She wiggled her brows and stroked the strained zipper of his jeans.

"I love you so much." Trevor unbuttoned her shirt all the way and pushed it off her shoulders. He bent his head and kissed where their baby grew. "I'll be the best father I can. I hope you know that."

"Damn straight. I'm teaching you to change diapers tomorrow." She giggled against his lips.

There would be time for working out the details later. Tonight, she was content to celebrate being engaged to the man who had walked off the silver screen and straight into her heart.

Epilogue

"HELLO, LADIES AND gentleman. Larry Quinton here and I have to tell you I'm in shock today. Only a couple weeks ago, my friend Trevor Jacobs was here to talk about his new movie." The host waited for the applause to die down. "As most people know, Trevor and I are friends off camera as well as on. But that rascal had a secret that not even I knew. We are starting the show off a little differently tonight because Trevor and his fiancée, yes, you heard that right, his *fiancée,* Kelly, are standing by to give us the scoop on this crazy chain of events that led him from being Hollywood's golden boy to Hollywood's rebel and now to being Hollywood's favorite source of gossip."

The screen changed to reveal Kelly and Trevor sitting on a couch together holding hands. Both had huge smiles on their faces even if Kelly's was slightly less sure.

"Hello lovebirds and might I say, Kelly, it's lovely to meet you. Congratulations on the baby. I hope you can make a trip out here once you are able."

The blonde beauty on the screen smiled brighter and her eyes finally sparkled. "Thank you, Larry, it's a pleasure to meet you too."

"Now I have to say, I'm in shock at this entire situation. It's not often anyone pulls off a secret in this industry and, Trevor, you have not only made a movie that has heads turning, you've also kept this relationship a huge secret. No offense, but anyone can see by looking at her that something was going on a few months ago." Larry chuckled and so did his audience.

Trevor delivered a well-rehearsed speech about how things unfolded. Some of the information was accurate and the rest was no one's business. In the end, both Kelly and Trevor came out looking like a couple that didn't want Hollywood to ruin the deep love they had for one another. It was well played on all counts. Larry bought it hook, line, and sinker, as did his audience.

The television host wasn't done yet. "Did I also hear correctly that Kelly was your muse for your latest movie?"

Trevor Jacobs looked over at his fiancée and gave her an adoring smile. "She's my muse in everything these days." The lovebirds were perfection together. "But, yes, Kelly's story was the inspiration for the film. Once I knew the other side of the coin, my perception of the whole idea changed. We both felt like her story needed to be told. It wasn't ideal for her because it dredged up some past pains, but we both agreed that if one woman can benefit from this movie, it was worth it."

"Kelly, how does it feel to have your story seen by millions of people?"

"I can't say I was too enthused about it at first. Trevor is full of surprises." She giggled and Trevor's cheeks reddened. "Once I realized the need to bring this issue to light, I got on board."

He leaned over and touched her belly affectionately. Kelly beamed up at Trevor. Her smile was radiant and the term "glowing" didn't do her justice.

"You two are so cute it's disgusting," Larry joked for his audience's sake. "It's refreshing to see you happy, Trevor."

"Thanks, Larry. I've been given an amazing gift."

"What's next for you guys? When's the baby due?"

"In about eight weeks."

"Boy or girl?"

"We don't know." Trevor shrugged and laughed. "You know us, we're full of surprises."

"As long as I'm the godfather. And the wedding?"

"Well, that would ruin all the fun if we told you, now wouldn't it?" Kelly laughed, finally feeling at ease in front of the camera.

"Fine, fine." Larry waved them off with both hands. The host exchanged goodbyes with his guests and turned back to the camera. "There you have it. I'm still in shock; I know you are too. There are millions of women weeping right now. Hell, I'm weeping. Did you see that woman? I wonder if she has a twin. Good job, Trevor. Wow! Goes to show you, folks sometimes you never know what's really going on behind the scenes. What a great story and I wish them the best.

"As if that wasn't exciting enough, when we come back we will have the man speaking out against Trevor's movie. Find out why he thinks bondage and BDSM is the spice of life. This could get freaky folks! Don't go away. We'll be back right after this commercial break—"

Pops turned off the television and leaned back in his recliner. He couldn't help but laugh. Who would have thought his granddaughter would be getting married to a movie star and starting a family worthy of gossip magazines? Boy, her parents would be proud. Trevor was a good young man.

He grinned to himself as he went into the sitting room where the camera crew packed up their gear from the broadcast. Trevor shook their hands and reminded them that they were under contract not to reveal their location.

Kelly waddled over to him and took his outstretched

hands. "How did it go?"

"Fabulous, sweetheart. You looked radiant and that Larry fellow sold the story for you."

"He was pretty helpful."

Trevor joined them, put his arms around her shoulders, and rubbed her stomach. "I have an idea," he announced. "Let's have the wedding here."

Pops thought about that for a long moment. He'd lived in this house his entire life and his parents before him. He thought of his beloved Nell and the son they lost. As he looked at Kelly's beautiful face, he saw both his son and his daughter-in-law in her features. They would have loved the idea, as would Nell.

"I think this old place can handle a wedding."

"The house is the reason we met." Kelly leaned in and kissed Trevor's cheek.

Pops chuckled to himself. "Yeah, I think you took that whole bed and breakfast thing way too far, son."

"I couldn't be happier that Mark lied his ass off."

"Damn punk." Pops shook his head, but he knew co-incidences didn't just happen. Some things were just meant to be.

Divine Awakening: The Divine Chronicles Book
1 by JoAnna Grace

A TREMOR WENT up her spine. Her breath became
lodged in her chest. She rubbed her sternum, hoping to re-
lieve the mysterious pressure. Avery looked up from the table she was clearing to see two men walk into her café. One
she recognized and one she didn't. It was the stranger who

captured her attention.

Even in a simple gray shirt he looked ready to take someone's head off. He had to be bordering on six and a half feet and his shoulders were as wide as a barn door. Not an inch of fat to be found. The cotton shirt stretched over every bulge and dip of his muscles. When deep brown eyes met hers, her pulse hiccupped, and she gasped.

The world froze. She couldn't help but stare, which was why she dropped the cup in her hands and sent it crashing to the floor. The mug shattered and coffee splashed everywhere. Idiot! She bent to clean up the mess. Why did she have to do something so clumsy in front of someone so handsome?

"Let me help you." Two large hands scooped up the pieces of the mug.

Avery's eyes shot up and met with the stranger's again. The staggering weight of his presence made her fall over. The minute her body started to shift, the man reached out and grabbed her elbow. A zing of current went up her arm. She would've fallen right on her ass.

"Easy there." When he spoke again, Avery swore that angels began to sing. His lips were delectably full and she watched them move. You should come with a warning label, Avery thought as she let out a nervous laugh. When he smiled and his cheeks tinted pink, she realized she'd said that out loud. Mortified, she jerked upwards and whopped her head on the table.

"Damn it!" She rubbed the sore spot. The delicious stranger stood and placed the pieces of the broken mug on her tray.

"Let me look at that. You might have a cut." Acting as if he owned the rights, he stepped in close and used his hands to tilt her head to see.

She stopped breathing for a moment. His hands were warm and soft on her skin. She could only imagine how they would feel when he touched a lover. The lustful thought made her suck in air. His scent nearly knocked her back to the floor. It was a combination of spring in the woods, hints of earth and crisp mountain air, and fresh rain on leaves. Notes of exotic spices that begged to be tasted and savored. Dear god, she wanted to roll in his scent until it was embedded into her pores.

"Great cologne," she whispered, because she didn't have much oxygen left.

"Oh." He looked from her head back to her eyes. His brows dipped. "I'm not wearing any. But thank you."

Damn. This man was dangerous with a capital D. Taking a step back, Avery tried like hell to gain her composure. Their whole interaction had only taken a minute.

"I'm fine. Really. Please have a seat and I'll be right with you." She gathered up the dirty and broken dishes and walked into the kitchen.

"Oh. My. God. That man is a walking orgasm inducer," Izzy, her best friend—and best employee—said as Avery closed her eyes for a moment. "I'm all hot and bothered, and he didn't even touch me. You must need a cigarette."

Avery chuckled and shook her head. "He's just a man, Izz. Just a man."

"Well let's pray that he's just a man that wants a feisty blonde woman to have his babies, shall we?" Izzy fluffed her corkscrew blonde hair and adjusted her top so her boobs were pushed up even higher. "C'mon girls, Mama needs a boyfriend."

"Izz. No."

Her friend blanched. "What? Why?"

"Cause I have dibbs." Avery and Izzy were still for a second before they both bolted for the door to the dining room. The minute they exited, they were composed except for the matching grins.

"Can I have the young, blue-eyed one at least?" Izzy

whispered and grabbed some menus.

"He's a new officer with Frank and Jerry. Keep that in mind." Both Frank and Jerry had claimed the girls as sisters and had a tendency to scare off any men who made a play at the girls.

"I think Mr. Muscle can take 'em both."

Avery sidled up to the table before Izzy, who winked as she walked on to the next group of customers. "G'morning. What can I get you gentleman?" Avery kept her eyes on the notepad in her hand. If she looked up, her brain might misfire again.

"Your name would be a great start."

Since that was the last damn thing she expected, Avery glanced up at the handsome stranger. Once again, her brain stopped working and she stood there with her mouth hanging open like a moron.

As if he noticed the awkward silence, the blue-eyed guy chuckled. "The bacon and egg platter for me, please. Over easy. No personal in- formation on the side."

Avery tried to smile or laugh or something except stare at the man who left her speechless. Dang, she had to get it together. She had a café to run here. With a slight head-shake, she focused on the man ordering. "Right. Bacon and eggs, over easy." She clarified and then turned to the flirt. "And what would you like to eat, sir?"

As soon as the words left her mouth, she regretted her phrasing. The man's eyes drifted down the length of her body and back up before he quirked a brow and tilted his head. He licked his bottom lip and Avery saw stars dance in her vision. One corner of his mouth pulled back. It didn't take a genius to figure out exactly what he was thinking. Her body went rigid. The apron over her chest was too tight. The heat in his eyes when he grinned was enough to set her insides on fire.

"From the menu," she spit out before he could say

something that made her blush more than she already was.

Get *Divine Awakening* at www.authorjoannagrace.
com or www.yandrpublishing.com

Did you like, or hopefully love *The Roles We Play*?
Did you know that authors need many reviews to help sales
and boosting of their pages online? Reviews can be two
sentences to multiple paragraphs.
Please consider leaving a review for this book at
http://amzn.to/29N1DPo

Thank you for thinking about helping an author. We really
appreciate reviews from readers and fans. You're awesome!!

ABOUT THE AUTHOR

JoAnna Grace lives in a world of alpha males and strong females where true love conquers all—at least in her writing! A proud indie, she has published The Divine Chronicles, the Blake Pride Series, and more. Joanna loves paranormal and urban fantasy romance novels. She's a romantic at heart.

From the time she started holding a crayon she began to create magical worlds. Living in the real world was never an option. JoAnna's tales are spun at her home in East Texas where she lives with her Prince Charming, three kids, and a couple dogs. When not hiding behind the computer screen chugging coffee, you can find her shopping. singing with the radio, or speaking on behalf of Y&R, a public relations and publishing company.

JoAnna Grace
Giving Wings to Words

BOOKS BY JOANNA GRACE

Divine Chronicle Series:
Divine Awakening
Divine Destiny
Divine Judgment
Divine Encounter
Divine Pursuit (Coming Soon)

The Roles We Play

Blake Pride Series:
Pride Before The Fall
Break Her Fall
The Harder They Fall
Divided We Fall (Coming Soon)

Omega Office Romance Series: *(Coming Soon)*
Crossing The Lines
Blurring The Lines
Erasing The Lines

FIND JOANNA ONLINE

Find JoAnna's Books online: www.authorjoannagrace.com
or www.yandrpublishing.com

Website: www.authorjoannagrace.com

Join JoAnna's group for monthly giveaways:
http://bit.ly/JoAnnaGrace

Email: authorjoannagrace@gmail.com

Social Media
Twitter: @JoAnnaGrace4ya
Facebook: Jo Anna Grace Author
Pinterest: JoGraceAuthor
Instagram: authorjoannagrace

Businesses for Authors & Readers
Reader's Boutique: www.readersboutique.com
Y&R PR: www.yandrpr.com
Y&R Publishing: www.yandrpublishing.com

www.ingramcontent.com/pod-product-compliance
Lightning Source LLC
Chambersburg PA
CBHW021100130626
46552CB00005B/2195